Books by Tom Hoffma...

*Paperback versions available online
at Amazon or Barnes & Noble*

Bartholomew the Adventurer • The Eleventh Ring

Bartholomew the Adventurer • The Thirteenth Monk

Bartholomew the Adventurer • The Seventh Medallion

•••

Orville Mouse and the Puzzle of the Clockwork Glowbirds

Orville Mouse and the Puzzle of the Shattered Abacus

Orville Mouse and the Puzzle of the Capricious Shadows

Orville Mouse and the Puzzle of the Last Metaphonium

Orville Mouse and the Puzzle of the Sagacious Sapling

•••

The Translucent Boy and the Girl Who Saw Him

The Translucent Boy and the Cat Who Ran Out of Time

The Translucent Boy and the Girl Who Dreamed She Could Fly

The Translucent Boy and the Man Who Walked to the Moon

The Translucent Boy and the Children of Ice

•••

The Comet Kid Chronicles • Under the Blue Comet

The Comet Kid Chronicles • The Unfocused Man

The Comet Kid Chronicles • The Sinister Sorcerer

THE TRANSLUCENT BOY

and the
children of ice

by Tom Hoffman

Tom Hoffman
Visit my website at thoffmanak.wordpress.com
Email: OrvilleMouse@gmail.com

Printed in the United States of America

First Printing: 2023
ISBN 978-1-7362816-9-7

For my amazing wife Alexis,
who has put up with my crazy
for over fifty years.
Love you always.

Table of Contents

For all the amazing
translucent kids out there
who spend their days
listening, reading,
and thinking.

"I knew when I met you
an adventure was
going to happen."

Winnie the Pooh

"We were together.
I forget the rest."

Walt Whitman

THE
TRANSLUCENT
BOY

and the
children of ice

Chapter 1

Angels Will Come

In the beginning, there was darkness, then a kind face, a gentle voice.

Her first memory was the sound of rustling pages turning, and little drawings; an apple, a bird, a cloud, a house, a spoon, a tree. There were others, but she had forgotten them.

As time passed, her awareness grew, the girl becoming mindful of the cozy cabin with its rough hewn wooden walls, the warm crackling stone fireplace, the intricate handwoven patterns of her soft woolen blanket, the deep silence of the forest that surrounded them.

Sometimes they would walk through the forest at night, their path illuminated by the light of a flickering lantern. The girl would stop, pointing to whatever caught her eye, looking up at her mother questioningly. Her mother would give it a name, satisfying for a moment the child's insatiable curiosity.

"Those are spruce trees, tall and strong, as you will be. They are home to the birds and squirrels. This is moss, soft, like your feather pillow. These are wild roses, full of grace and beauty, just as you are."

When she was three, the girl found a cracked and badly tarnished mirror on the wooden table next to her mother's bed. She stared silently at her crooked reflection, then carried the mirror outside to her mother.

"Green eyes."

Her mother smiled. "How clever you are. Yes, your eyes are green, the color of budding leaves in the springtime. You gazed upon the trees until your eyes turned such a glorious shade of green."

The girl pointed to her hair. "White hair."

Her mother nodded. "You frolicked in the sparkling winter snow, your hair turning white, just as mine did when I grew old."

When she was eight, she was hunting for herbs in the forest and spotted a white fox peering out from behind a gnarled old spruce tree. She stared at him silently, listening, then offered him bread and cheese and her eternal friendship. Fox took up residence under their small porch, becoming her trusted companion, her ever vigilant guardian. She would gently pet his soft white fur, scratching his pointy ears, speaking to him with her thoughts, sharing her secrets with him.

Sometimes he would come into the house and lie quietly on the floor next to her while she practiced her reading, her mother listening as she sewed, correcting any mistakes the girl might make.

"One day you will be able to read all the books in the wooden chest. Such grand tales of adventure await you."

The girl furrowed her brow, asking her mother, "Are the people we read about real? Are they like you and like me?"

Her mother shook her head. "They are not real, they are fictional characters, living only in our imagination."

It wasn't until later that night, when she was safely tucked into her soft bed, Fox sleeping soundly on his woven rug, that the girl wondered about the people who had written the books. Were they real, like her and her mother and Fox? Did the Others write the books?

Three times a year, after tucking the girl's long white hair securely under a dark woolen cap, mother and daughter would make the long trek through the forest to the village of the Others.

The girl's mother had two steadfast, unwavering rules for her during their visits to the village. Under no circumstances was she to open her eyes, and she must never speak. She warned the girl in her strictest voice that if she opened her eyes, even once, just for a quick look, the angels would come and take her away. This frightened the girl beyond measure, and not once did she disobey her mother's instruction. In the village, she heard her mother tell the Others that the child was blind and could not speak.

When they left the village, once again nestled in the long purple shadows of the towering spruce trees, her mother would show her what she had purchased from the Others, never failing to produce a small cloth bag of sweets for the girl. "You did well, dear one, the angels will not be coming for you today."

When she was twelve, the girl told her mother that she wanted to see the Others with her own eyes, just as her mother saw them. Perhaps she could make friends with them and they would not tell the angels she had opened her eyes or spoken.

Her mother shook her head. "I'm sorry, dear one, the Others are not like us, and they are not like Fox. They are filled with darkness, fear, and anger, destroying what they do not understand. The angels would come and take you away from me."

The girl thought for a long time, then said, "Do the Others have green eyes and white hair as I do?"

"They do not."

When she was fourteen, the girl said to her mother, "Fox and I are going to hunt for herbs in the forest. He will keep me safe. No one will see us in the darkness."

"Take the lantern and don't go far, the forest can be a dangerous place, even without threat of the Others."

"Fox will protect me from all harm."

She headed off into the woods, Fox trotting along next to her. She sent her thoughts to Fox. *"We are not hunting for herbs. We are going to the village. I want to see the*

6

Others. I am of a proper age now to see them. We'll walk to the edge of the forest and I shall peek through the trees. It is time."

Fox stared at her silently, his expression unreadable.

An hour later they arrived at the edge of the forest, the girl studying carefully a series of low wooden buildings, dimly lit by the light of a crescent moon. The girl extinguished her lantern, peering cautiously through the trees into the ominous uncertainty of the village.

"I am a moth, the village an irresistible flame."

Fox stared silently at the girl.

"I can see their silhouettes, but I must get closer. I want to see their faces. I want to see their eyes."

Fox was searching the village for signs of danger.

The girl crept forward, being careful not to step on any dry twigs that might give her away, giving a yelp of surprise when a boy stepped out from a wooden shed holding a glowing lantern. He stared at her, his eyes widening, fear suddenly flooding across his face, his cries echoing through the village.

"FOREST WITCH! ALL BEWARE THE FOREST WITCH!"

Two shadowy figures darted out of a wooden building, one of them carrying a long deadly musket. There was a flash of light, a thundering boom, a lead ball splintering a branch next to the girl. She turned and ran, her heart pounding, Fox racing after her, the pair of friends retreating back to the silence and safety of the ghostly black forest.

When she returned to their cabin, the girl made no mention to her mother of their visit to the village of the Others. She was of a proper age to see them, even if it put her in danger. Fox would protect her from all harm. She knew this to be an indisputable truth.

Chapter 2

African Violets

Odo Whitley woke up on Saturday morning with a grin on his face. He and his best friend Sephie Crumb were taking their tour of Pravus University today, the two them having decided to attend the same college after they graduated in the spring. Odo would study physics, Sephie would study engineering. Pravus University was their obvious choice, as it was relatively affordable, close to home, and had highly respected programs in both physics and engineering.

Odo pressed his hand against the bedroom wall, using his remarkable translucent powers to make a small section of it transparent. He peered through the wall at a clear blue sky.

"Nice and sunny, a perfect day for the tour. This is going to be so much fun. We'll take the twelve o'clock bus and get there early so we won't miss the tour. I don't want to be late."

He flopped back on his pillow, his thoughts turning to

Sephie and their recent adventures on Varania with Silas and Emmy, the other two members of the Odd Squad. Each of the Odd Squad members possessed certain remarkable powers; Odo was translucent and could walk through walls, Sephie was half Fortisian and could scan people's brainwaves and shape physical objects using her mind, Silas could see ghosts and sometimes talk to them, and Emmy could fly, transforming her physical body into a dream body.

Odo and Sephie were also proficient shifters, able to travel to other worlds using waystones and the power of their minds. Wikerus Praevian had taught them that a waystone was nothing more than an object originating from another world.

Odo was also remembering the challenge recently given to him by Mike the Mechanic, a mysterious and exceedingly annoying being who existed simultaneously on thousands of different worlds. Mike the Mechanic had asked Odo if he loved Sephie, demanding a simple yes or no answer to win the challenge. Odo had surprised himself, answering yes, and Mike the Mechanic had confirmed that Odo's answer was correct. Despite Odo's realization that he did indeed love Sephie, he had not yet told her, unable to find the perfect moment.

His meandering thoughts were interrupted by a slamming door, most likely Odo's dad leaving for work, having recently been promoted to a senior manager position at the Chocko CrunchCakes Corporation.

"Time to get up." He hopped out of bed, throwing on his clothes, then hesitated, eyeing his tall wooden dresser.

"Maybe I should wear my work ring and see what happens on the tour. It might help us get accepted at Pravus. We might meet someone."

He pulled open his sock drawer, rummaging around until he found a small black box. Flipping it open, he removed the gleaming silver ring with its small inscription on the inner surface, *aperi oculos tuos et vide*. Sephie had translated the Latin words for him; *open your eyes and see*.

Mrs. Preke, the administrative assistant at the Serendipity Salvage Company and a formshifting Plindorian alien, had given Odo the ring when she hired him at Serendipity Salvage. She told him to wear it whenever he wanted to work, and remove it when he was done. It had taken him some time to realize that the ring was the cause of remarkably unusual coincidences, leading him to unforeseen destinations, often meeting new people or finding curious unlikely objects. The first time he wore the ring was the first time he had talked to Sephie, and the first time he had ever talked to a girl.

He slipped the ring onto his finger and darted down the stairs. As he stepped into the kitchen he called out, "Odo Whitley is in the house! All hail King Odo!" Announcing his presence had become a daily ritual for Odo, a ritual that began the morning he walked into the kitchen while his parents were arguing, neither of them noticing their translucent son, saying things he knew they did not want him to hear.

Petunia Whitley, his mom, rolled her eyes. "I heard you coming down the stairs. You don't need to shout every time you walk into the kitchen. I can see you if I focus on you."

"Just wanted to make sure you knew I was here. Did Dad go to work? I heard the front door slam. Is everything okay?"

"They're having problems at the factory, he said something about the Golden CrunchCake ovens not working."

"Do you think he'll go back to school like you did? Get a degree?"

"I don't know, his job keeps him busy and he's making a good living now that he's a senior manager. He likes his job."

"Sephie and I have our tour of Pravus today. I can't wait to see what their physics department is like. It's going to be so fun."

"Your tour is today? I thought it was tomorrow. I promised Mrs. Beasley you'd help her today. I'm so sorry, but you have to cancel your tour."

Odo stared blankly at his mom. "I can't cancel it. Sephie's going with me. I can't miss it. We want to go together."

"You can both go next weekend, I'll make it up to you.

You have to help Mrs. Beasley today. It's very important, I promised her. There's no one else who can help her."

Odo felt his jaw tightening, his anger growing. It was a feeling he didn't like, and a feeling that faded away the moment he realized his work ring was more than likely responsible for this unexpected and unwanted turn of events. It wasn't the first time this had happened.

"What does she want? More help with her giant dog?"

His mom laughed. "Isn't Tiny something?"

"Something like a horse that drools."

"I know he's big, but Mrs. Beasley loves him."

"What does she need help with?"

"You need to help her take all her African violets to the Bedford Falls Annual Flower Show."

Odo's heart sank down to the center of the earth. "I have to go to a flower show? Seriously? A flower show?"

"It will be lovely, they have all kinds of flowers there."

Odo twisted his ring around his finger, glaring at it. Why was it doing this? What could possibly happen at a dumb flower show?

"Odo?"

"What time do I have to be at Mrs. Beasley's?"

"In one hour."

"How many African violets does she have?"

His mom made a funny face. "She loves African violets almost as much as she loves Tiny."

"So she has a billion of them. Great."

"I have to go or I'll be late for my Medieval Literature class. It's very interesting. Did you know they had children's books in the middle ages? They were used to teach children acceptable behavior, or how to read and write. It's quite interesting."

"No fantasy adventure stories?"

Petunia laughed. "Don't forget Mrs. Beasley."

"I won't. Have fun at school."

Exactly nine minutes later, Odo's phone buzzed. It was Sephie. He groaned. This was not going to be fun, she was going to be upset about him canceling their tour.

"Hey, Seph, what's up?"

"No college tour today. The university called and said the guide is sick, but they rescheduled us for next weekend."

Odo blinked. This was another completely unexpected turn of events. "Are you wearing your work ring?"

"How did you know that? I thought we might meet someone special on our tour."

"I thought the same thing, but when I put it on my mom said I had to cancel the tour because she promised Mrs. Beasley I would help her today."

"Both our rings cancelled the tour. That's interesting. What do you think it means?"

"I think it means I have to help Mrs. Beasley drag a billion African violets to the Bedford Falls Flower Show."

"The flower show? You're lucky, they have beautiful flowers there. I'll go with you. It will be fun. I'd love to see it."

"That would be great. How soon can you be here?"

"Fifteen minutes. See you."

Thirty-nine minutes later Odo was knocking on Mrs. Beasley's front door, Sephie standing next to him.

"Watch out for her insane giant dog Tiny, he drools like a broken fire hydrant."

Sephie snorted. "I can shape you a shiny yellow raincoat if you want."

The door swung open, Mrs. Beasley giving them a cheery smile, her eyes on Sephie. "You must be Sephie. My goodness, Petunia was right, you are beautiful. I love your orange hair, it's quite fetching."

"Odo's mom said I was beautiful?" Sephie glanced at Odo.

"She did indeed, and she was quite right." She lowered her voice to barely above a whisper, looking around as though someone might overhear her. "*She also told me why Odo is translucent. It was the perfume she got in the mail.*" She raised her eyebrows.

Odo laughed. "You don't have to whisper, I don't mind being translucent. I'm used to it and I kind of like it now. It's not embarrassing at all."

"That's wonderfully brave of you, and thank you so much for helping me today. Some of the trays are very heavy and I have rather bad arthritis in my hands. It can be quite painful. Such a dreadful nuisance."

Sephie said, "We're happy to help. The flower show sounds like so much fun. I can't wait to see it."

Odo peered in through the doorway. "Right. Where are all the African violets?"

Mrs. Beasley motioned for them to come in. "I'm afraid you're going to think I'm a little batty in the belfry about my African violets."

Chapter 3

The Flower Show

Odo and Sephie stepped inside, Odo scanning the room for Mrs. Beasley's giant dog. "Where's Tiny?"

"He's staying with the neighbors while I'm at the flower show. You can run over and say hello to him if you'd like, he's just next door."

"Um… that's okay, he's a great dog, but we don't want to be late for the show."

Sephie couldn't help herself. "You're sure you don't want to go see him, Odo? Give him a big hug?"

Odo gave her an excessively pleasant smile. "We don't want to be late for the show, Sephie."

Mrs. Beasley nodded. "Odo's right, we should get cracking, load up the car. Follow me."

She headed down the hallway, pointing to a pale green door. "They're in the garage."

Odo's eyes widened when she opened the door.

"Whoa, what is all this stuff?"

"It's a computer controlled watering system with timed, self-adjusting grow lights for each variety of

African violet. I'm quite proud of it, I installed most of it myself. "

Odo studied the complex system of hoses and lights. "That's actually pretty cool. You really do have a lot of African violets."

Mrs. Beasley nodded. "It's a little embarrassing that I have so many, but I do love them. They're so delicate and so pretty."

Sephie strolled around the garage, admiring the flowers. "They're beautiful, and so many different kinds of them."

"Last year I won a gold medal for most varieties of a single flower. I keep it on my mantlepiece."

"Very nice. How many kinds of African violets are there?"

Odo could feel his stomach twisting into a painful knot. Why was Sephie asking questions about the flowers? What was she thinking? "We should probably get busy moving stuff if we want to get–"

Mrs. Beasley answered Sephie, saying, "That's a wonderful question, Sephie. African violets come in a wide range of colors and forms, several hundred varieties in fact, depending upon the flower color, shape, and size of the plant."

Odo felt a creeping desperation growing inside him. Things were going downhill fast, and Sephie wasn't helping.

Mrs. Beasley continued. "It's quite fascinating how

the flower colors vary from blue to violet, lavender, pink, red-violet, blue-violet, lavender-pink and white. The shapes of the flowers vary also. They can be single, double, semi-double, star-shaped, fringed or ruffled. Some varieties have flowers where two or more rows of petals are one color, and the other petals are fringed in a different color. It's all quite lovely, almost magical."

Odo was shifting his weight from one foot to the other. This was bad.

Sephie said, "It's amazing that one flower can have so many different forms."

"Isn't it? And that's just the blossoms. The leaf shapes are quite varied also. They can be plain, quilted, spidered, ruffled, fringed, scalloped, spooned, pointed or variegated."

Sophie grinned. "They're all so beautiful."

Odo saw an opening and made his move. "We don't want to miss the show. Which flowers go in the car?"

"The racks in the back of my car will hold ten trays of flowers. I've put a bright yellow sticker on each tray that needs to go."

Mrs. Beasley opened the garage door, her car already in position. She raised the rear door, pointing to the racks. "Each rack holds five trays."

Odo surreptitiously glanced at his watch. This was going to be the longest day in the history of the universe.

After driving for half an hour and hunting for a parking spot at the crowded convention center, they loaded the trays of flowers onto carts and headed into the show.

Mrs. Beasley said, "I reserved five tables for my display, R12 through R16."

"Got it." Odo spotted the sign for Row R and twenty-five minutes later Mrs. Beasley's African violets were on display for all to see.

She clasped her hands together, beaming at Odo and Sephie. "Thank you so much for all your help. Odo, I know this isn't much fun for you, so please know how much I appreciate your help. This means so much to me, and I couldn't have done it by myself with my dreadful arthritis."

Odo gave his best sincerely puzzled look. "I'm not bored at all, I think your flowers are amazing."

Sephie laughed, grinning at Mrs. Beasley, then said to Odo, "Let's look around for an hour, then take the bus home. I want to see everything. One hour, then we go."

"I was thinking we should probably head back to–"

"Maybe we'll find something amazing here. Wouldn't that be nice?"

Odo eyed his work ring. Sephie was right, they had no idea why their rings had sent them to the flower show. They couldn't leave until they knew the reason.

As they headed off down the aisle, Odo said, "One hour, then we go. Let's split up and look around, see if we find anything interesting. Meet up in twenty minutes."

"Text me if you find something."

Odo strolled around the show, looking for anyone or anything that might not be what it appeared to be. "Maybe I'll meet a formshifting alien, or maybe a wizard with a key to a lost gold temple, or a mysterious old–" He froze when he heard a familiar voice call his name.

"Odo! What are you doing here?"

He spun around. "Silas? Emmy? What are you guys doing here?"

Silas and Emmy darted over to him, Silas whispering, "Our work rings sent us here. I think we're supposed to find something, but we don't know what. All I see are a billion flowers."

"Sephie's here. Our rings sent us here too. We had to cancel our tour of Pravus."

Emmy whispered, "Have you found anything yet? We just got here. What are we looking for?"

"It's probably nothing, but I did see a Sinarian walking around with a glowing green orb floating in front of him."

Emmy burst out laughing. "You're so funny."

Silas rolled his eyes. "Funny looking."

"Let's split up and look around. Sephie's looking too. Text if you find something."

Odo continued on down the aisle, stopping when he reached the far corner of the convention center's main room, his eyes on a display table void of flowers, a man hunched over in his chair reading a magazine, the table covered with an array of curious antiques. Odo knew

21

he'd found what he was looking for when the man looked up, revealing his face. It was Jonathan Morse, the eccentric and extremely knowledgeable antique dealer who had helped them identify numerous objects during the course of their adventures. Odo rubbed his hands together. Jonathan Morse was why the rings had brought them here. "Bingo!"

Chapter 4

The Sampler

Odo waved to Jonathan, stepping over to his table. "What are you doing at a flower show?"

Jonathan eyed Odo with his usual dry expression. "I was just wondering why so many people were bringing flowers to an antique show. Now I know. My bad."

Odo laughed. "You're selling antiques here?"

Jonathan shrugged. "Flower people like antiques, especially old vases like these ones, and old gardening tools. They decorate their houses with them. I do pretty well here."

"That makes sense." Odo scanned the cluttered table, searching for whatever it was that he was supposed to find. He was getting an odd feeling. "What's all that stuff?"

"It's not stuff, those are original antique needlework samplers, many of them with quite charming designs. They're popular at garden shows, big sellers, especially the ones with flowers."

"What were they for?"

"It was a way for people to demonstrate their proficiency in needlework. Most were done by schoolgirls back in the day. Many of them have alphabets, figures, numbers, and decorative borders. They usually have the name of the person who embroidered it and the date they made it. Some are extremely valuable, some are not."

Odo was surprised by his inexplicable fascination with the samplers. This was curious, because it wasn't something he would normally be drawn to.

"Can I look through them?"

Jonathan shrugged. "Knock yourself out. Not many young folks take an interest in them."

"They're kind of cool." Odo carefully studied each sampler, looking for clues. He stopped when he saw the last one, unable to take his eyes off it, an eerie chill running through him. The sampler wasn't elaborate, it had no flowers, just a house, a figure next to the house, two trees, and two people carrying lanterns. The border was made of letters, but it wasn't the alphabet, just a string of random letters. He held it up to Jonathan Morse. "What do you know about this one?"

"I know it's not a very good one. Plain, very basic needlework, self-taught I should imagine, no flowers, letters are a confusing jumble at best. The valuable ones have a pretty scene. This one is old, though. You can date them from the style of stitches used. These letters are done with eyelet stitches and satin stitches, popular in the first half of the eighteenth century. By 1790 most people were using cross-stitches." He studied it closely, pointing to the lower left corner. "There it is, 1749. That's when it was made."

"Whoa, that's super old. It must be worth a lot."

"Age doesn't always translate into value. Just ask any old person." He gave his signature dry laugh.

Odo gave a start when someone brushed up against him. It was Sephie. Her eyes were bright, focused on the sampler he was holding. "You found something."

"It's a sampler made in 1749."

"It's lovely. I think you should buy it. I've been looking for something exactly like that."

"Really?"

"Really."

Seconds later Silas and Emmy appeared. Silas studied the sampler. "That's super cool, you should get that."

Emmy nodded. "It's very cool, I like it. You really should get it."

Odo turned to Jonathan. "How much is it?"

Jonathan eyed the four friends curiously. "You all want to buy an old sampler made in 1749?"

Odo nodded. "It's super cool."

Jonathan leaned back in his chair, studying the four young friends. "I could let it go for four thousand dollars."

"What? Are you serious? Four thousand dollars?"

"Or I could let it go for a hundred and fifty. I've had it for over a year without a nibble. That's a fair price."

Odo looked at Sephie. She nodded. "We'll take it. Pay him, Odo."

"How come I have to-"

"Time is money, Odo Whitley. Pay him."

Odo reached into his pocket, pulling out his wallet. "I was going to put this in the bank to help pay for my college tuition."

Jonathan gave a groan. "And he plays the saving for college tuition card. Shrewd. Fine, you can have it for one hundred dollars, but that's it, not a penny less."

Odo pulled a crisp one hundred dollar bill from his wallet, handing it to Jonathan. "Thanks, I appreciate it."

Jonathan handed the sampler to Odo. "Pleasure doing business. Always interesting when you show up. You're an odd bunch of kids, I'll give you that. A lot more to you than meets the eye, I'll wager."

Odo laughed, the friends heading off across the convention center, exiting through the main doors, making their way to the bus stop.

Silas said, "Why do you think we all wanted to buy the sampler?"

"It must be important, maybe it's a map or something."

Silas studied the sampler, eyeing the border of jumbled letters. "Those letters could mean something."

"Like she never learned the alphabet?"

"Maybe it's a secret code."

"It could be the coordinates for a lost treasure worth

millions."

Sephie said, "That's not what the rings do, Odo. You know that."

"Maybe the house and the people mean something. Do you think we're supposed to find the house?"

"How could we possibly find it? We don't even know where the sampler was made. Besides, there's no way a little wooden house in 1749 would still be around."

"Good point. I'll take it home and try to decipher the letters. It could be a code, or it could be in another language."

Silas said, "Maybe it's an alien language."

Odo looked dubious. "You're saying you think an alien embroidered this in 1749?"

"You never know, aliens might like embroidering."

"Right." Odo pulled out his phone and took a picture of the sampler, texting it to the others. "Everyone study the sampler tonight, look for clues, see if you can figure anything out. We'll meet at lunch tomorrow."

The friends headed their separate ways, Odo studying the sampler on the way home, discovering nothing new.

That evening after dinner, he headed up to his room with the sampler, setting it on his desk, examining it carefully with his big magnifying glass.

"Jonathan Morse said it was an authentic eighteenth century sampler, but there was nothing unusual about it. He said it wasn't especially well crafted, the person who made it was more than likely self taught. The jumbled letters could be some kind of code though, or it could be in another language."

He copied the letters onto a piece of paper, trying to make sense of them.

m e r e d u c e n t i n v e r a m d o m u m a n g e l i

"It's weird, whatever it is. It kind of looks like words, but it doesn't make any sense. Maybe it's French, or Italian. I see the word *angel* in it, but it also could be *mangeli* or *mumangeli*, whatever that means. That sounds kind of like Italian. I should look up mangeli, see if that's a word. I wish I knew someone who spoke–"

A light blinked on in Odo's head. "It's not Italian, it's Latin, just like the inscription on my ring!" He grabbed his phone and texted Sephie.

I think the letters on the sampler are in Latin! Can you translate it? mereducentinveramdomumangeli

Sephie replied a few moments later.

Way ahead of you, Odo. You started in the wrong place. It should read, angeli me reducent in veram domun

What does that mean?

28

It means the angels will carry me back to my true home

Odo stared silently at Sephie's text, then texted his reply.

What does that mean?

It means the angels will carry her back to her true home.

Odo was imagining the smirky grin on Sephie's face.

Hilarious. See you tomorrow.

He slumped back in his chair, staring at the sampler. "Whoever embroidered this is probably saying the angels will take her to heaven when she dies, back to her true home. That would make sense, since the sampler was made back in 1749, back when people thought angels had wings and heaven was–" Odo never finished his thought, his startled eyes focused like white hot burning lasers on the sampler, an icy chill rushing through him.

"Not possible. No way. Am I going loopy?"

He grabbed his phone, scrolling down to the photo of the sampler he had taken at the flower show, studying it. He wasn't going loopy. It was impossible, but he was right. In the photograph he took, there were two people carrying lanterns, but on the sampler sitting in front of him, there were three people carrying lanterns.

Chapter 5

The Villagers

The white-haired girl was kneeling in the garden, digging potatoes with a wooden trowel when she heard a rustling sound coming from the woods. Fox spun around, letting out a shrill bark. The girl turned just in time to see a rough looking man with dark hair and a long dark beard running off. She knew he was one of the Others. She raced into the house to tell her mother.

"There was someone in the woods! They saw me and ran away. It was a person with dark hair and a long beard."

Her mother sank down onto a chair. "My greatest fear has been realized. It won't be long before they come for us. I have dreaded this day for so many years."

"We have to leave, run away, before they come back. Will the angels take me away? He saw my white hair. I don't want them to take me. We have to leave so the angels won't find me."

"The angels do not wish us to leave. They will protect us."

"How do you know that?"

"An angel spoke to me in my thoughts."

Solis studied her mother's face. "An angel spoke to you the same way I speak with Fox?"

Her mother nodded. "It was many years ago, but the memory of it is sharp and clear, as though it were yesterday."

"Even so, we must leave our home. The villagers will come and destroy us."

"The angels will protect us. You will protect us. It has been foretold by the angel."

Solis was remembering the deadly loud weapon the Others had used at the village. She knew there was no defense against such a device as that, but she dared not mention her knowledge of the weapon to her mother, dared not mention that she had seen the village of the Others.

The forest was eerily silent as the sun dipped below the treeline, the long purple shadows stretching across their yard. Solis sat at the small window, her eyes scanning the forest. Her mother was in her rocking chair, sewing.

Solis called out when she saw the flickering lights. "I can see them! They have torches. There are at least a dozen of them. They have long iron weapons."

"They are called muskets. They kill from a great distance, firing a round ball made of lead."

"What should we do? Suppose they set fire to our

house with their torches?"

"You will protect us, just as the angel said you would."

"I can't protect us, I'm a child. They have muskets and torches. They will destroy us."

"You are a child born of angels, dear one."

A voice rang out from the forest. "FOREST WITCH, SHOW YOURSELF!"

Fox spoke to Solis in her thoughts.

"You must face them. In your heart, you know this to be true."

"You are certain?"

"You already know my answer."

Solis was terrified, but Fox was right. She had to confront them, even if it meant her own death. The angels would take her back to her true home. She opened the front door, stepping out onto the porch, Fox standing next to her.

"I AM NOT A FOREST WITCH! I AM A PERSON, JUST AS YOU ARE."

One of the villagers stepped forward, a long deadly musket in his hands.

"Your witch hair and witch eyes tell a different story, evil one! Your vile lies fall upon our deaf ears. I shall send you back to the darkness from which you sprang, witch!"

The villager raised his musket, aiming it directly at her. Solis didn't move, but Fox did. With a shrill bark he raced across the grass toward the villager. There was a flash of light, a thundering boom, and Fox tumbled to the ground, lying motionless in the grass.

Solis stared at Fox in disbelief, her body numb, her thoughts vanishing. She didn't hear the primordial howl of anguish that poured out of her. She grabbed her head, letting out a low moan. Something was happening, something she didn't understand, a terrifying unknown force coursing through her body. She was dying, the angels were taking her away. She held out both hands, palms facing outward, unaware of her own actions, blinded by the sight of dear Fox lying dead in the grass, his white fur stained with a dreadful crimson color.

There was an eerie crackling noise, sparkling ice crystals forming, glinting brightly in the night air, the ground suddenly covered with thick hoarfrost, a numbing, bitter arctic wind howling toward the villagers.

They screamed when it hit them, the rosy color in their cheeks draining away, their torches extinguished, the iron muskets frozen to their hands. They staggered back, the bitterly icy wind viciously biting their flesh, gnawing at their bones. They screamed out in terror, stumbling off into the forest. Then they were gone, the forest silent again.

Solis fell to her knees. Two tall spruce trees above her erupted into a ball of fiery orange flames, the branches crackling wildly, ten thousand glowing sparks shooting up into the night sky. She gazed up at the trees, watching the flames vanish, her body glowing with a brilliant orange light. She was cradling Fox in her arms, tears streaming down her face, watching as his body faded away like morning fog in the warm sun, her arms suddenly empty. He was gone.

Her mother was there, reaching down, helping Solis to her feet.

The words poured out of Solis' mouth. "You saw? You saw what I did? You saw what they did to Fox? They killed my dearest friend. They killed him for no reason!"

"I saw, dear one."

"Where did Fox go? What happened to him? What have I done? Why did it get so cold?"

"The angels took your dear Fox to heaven, child."

"I didn't see any angels. Where is he? Where did he go? I want him to come back."

"Come into the house, there is something I must show you."

Solis stepped into the cabin, her body still shaking. She took a seat at the crudely fashioned wooden table, her eyes on the small well worn rug where Fox always slept. Fox was gone, he would never sleep there again. She would never awaken in the morning and reach down to pet his soft white fur.

Her mother set a small crystal box on the table, taking a seat across from Solis.

"The angel told me this day would come. I raised you from an infant, but you are not of my own blood, dear one. An angel brought you to me. I saw him as clearly as I am seeing you this very moment. He came down from the heavens in a brilliant sphere of white light as I stood watching. The angel was like nothing I have ever seen, as white as the driven snow. He was holding the hand of a child with snow white hair and bright green eyes. When he looked at me I was filled with a peace and joy unknown to me until that moment. He spoke to me not with words, but with his thoughts, as you speak to Fox. He told me to raise you, to care for you, to love you as my own, and told me that one day you would leave, that you were destined to become a great and noble savior. He gave me this crystal box, telling me to keep it safe, that in time you would need the contents. You, dear one, are a child born of angels, and that is why your hair is snow white, and that is why your eyes are the color of new leaves in the spring."

"I don't understand. Where did the frost and ice and fire come from?"

"They came from you. The power of the angels is yours." Her mother slid the crystal box gently toward Solis.

"You may open it. It is your birthright."

Solis slowly raised the lid of the box, peering into it.

"It is a medallion. Why does it glow with such a curious light?"

"It glows with the eternal light of the angels."

Solis awoke the next morning, her heart filled with an

inconsolable grief when she remembered Fox was gone. "What shall I do without dear Fox? I am lost in this world."

Her mother answered, "I am old, and in my day I have seen many souls pass on to the heavenly realm. You must continue steadfastly onward until it is your time to pass. Be brave, dear Solis, for the grandest of all adventures await you."

Solis got up, stepping over to a small wooden chest, taking out a square of linen cloth, six spools of colored thread, and a silver needle.

"I shall honor my dearest friend Fox, and he will live forever."

Chapter 6

Threads of Time

"Seriously, look at the photo, then look at the sampler." Odo set the sampler down on the cafeteria table, the others studying it curiously.

"What about it? We've already seen the sampler."

"You don't see the difference?"

Silas gave a start. "There are four people with lanterns, or torches, maybe."

"What?" Odo spun it around, looking at it. "There's a new one. Last night there were three, now there are four."

Emmy said, "How is that possible?"

Silas shrugged. "It was probably embroidered by an evil wizard with a pet dragon."

Odo ignored him, drumming his fingers on the table. "It's some kind of scientific phenomenon that we don't understand."

"That narrows it down. Wait, did you see any elves in your room last night?"

Emmy snickered. "Good one. Elves."

"Yes, very funny, I get it, elves did it. We need to take

this to Wikerus. I have no idea what's causing this."

Silas eyed the sampler, scrunching up his face. "It could be temporal nonlocality."

Odo frowned. "Temporal what?"

"It's like quantum entanglement, but across time. It's a thing in physics. Temporal nonlocality."

Emmy said, "What does it mean?"

"Quantum entanglement is when particles are connected across space, but temporal nonlocality is when particles are connected across time. The sampler might exist simultaneously in different times, in the now of 1749 and in the now that we are living in."

"Is that how Mike the Mechanic can live on all those worlds at the same time?"

"Maybe. They don't really understand how it all works yet."

Sephie said, "Are you saying we're watching someone back in 1749 embroider the sampler?"

"Maybe. What else could it be?"

Odo stared at the sampler. "This is definitely weird. We should show it to Wikerus."

Sephie nodded her agreement. "It's odd that all of us were drawn to the flower show and to the sampler. That's never happened before. This must be something really important."

"Let's take the bus to my house after school and we'll go see Wikerus."

Emmy said, "Keep checking the sampler for

changes."

"Are you taking your tour of Pravus this weekend?"

"We are, and I can't wait. They have a super good physics department, all kinds of cool research going on there."

"Maybe they could tell us what's happening with the sampler."

"They'd ask too many questions and we'd wind up prisoners in a secret government facility."

"Good point."

The lunch bell rang, the four friends heading off to their classes. "Don't forget, we're all taking the bus to Odo's after school."

That afternoon found the four friends strolling down Expergo Street, heading to the home of the mysterious formshifting Fortisian, Wikerus Praevian. It was Wikerus who had told Sephie her birth parents had died at the hands of Stirpian invaders, and that her father had been a Fortisian, and the source of her unusual powers.

Silas said, "Hey, Odo, did you ever do anything with that T-Rex tooth that Harold gave you?"

"It's in my sock drawer. What do you think Harold is doing now? I miss him."

"He's having fun somewhere in Pangaea taking pictures of dinosaurs."

"That sounds so cool. I wish we were back there."

"I remember how much you liked that Spinosaurus."

"I wasn't scared of it, just surprised by the look of it."

"Right. Harold said you could clone a T-Rex from the DNA in the tooth, that it wasn't a fossil, it was a real tooth."

"That's my senior science fair project. I'm bringing a full grown T-Rex to school."

Emmy laughed. "Make sure it's on a leash."

"Here we are." Sephie ran up the steps to Wikerus Praevian's spooky looking Victorian mansion, knocking on the door. It opened moments later, a smiling middle aged woman wearing an ill fitting gray dress peering out. "There you are, Wikerus has been expecting you."

"He knew we were coming?"

"Well, you know, it's been a while since you've stopped by. Do come in."

The four friends stepped into the house, eyeing the elegant interior of the magnificent home.

Silas said, "Are those paintings real?"

Emmy gasped. "Is that an original Monet?"

"Wikerus bought that from Claude Monet in the spring of 1892."

"Wikerus knew Monet? Wait, did he temporal shift back there?"

"Of course he did, he's not *that* old." Mrs. Preke laughed.

They stepped into the sitting room, Wikerus waving to them from his ornately carved stuffed armchair. He pointed to two open boxes of imported Belgian chocolates on the table. "Just for you. Lots of orange creams."

"You knew we were coming?"

"I had a hunch. Do you have something to show me? A baffling mystery that needs unraveling?"

Silas said, "We have an embroidered sampler that might exist simultaneously in two different times."

"Most intriguing. It becomes a far more complex issue if you consider the fact that time is more illusion than reality."

Odo nodded, glancing at Sephie. "Right, an illusion. Anyway, we have this sampler that keeps changing, as though we're watching someone embroider it across time."

"When was it made?"

"In 1749. Jonathan Morse the antique dealer told us all about it."

"Interesting year, 1749."

"Why?"

"Why what?"

"Why is 1749 an interesting year?"

"Show me the sampler."

Odo took it from his backpack, setting it down on the table next to Wikerus. Mrs. Preke stepped over to it, gently pressing her palm against it. "Oh, my." She looked at Wikerus, raising her eyebrows.

Sephie said, "What is it?"

"It's just a lovely sampler, that's all. Very old."

Odo's eyes narrowed. He couldn't read brain waves like Sephie could, but he didn't have to. Mrs. Preke and

Wikerus were totally hiding something.

Sephie said, "We think it's important, because our work rings led all four of us to the sampler at the Bedford Falls Flower Show. We all knew we had to have it."

"Not surprising, it's very powerful."

"What do you mean?"

Wikerus hesitated. "I can tell you this much. The person who is embroidering this is a most remarkable being indeed."

"They have powers?"

"Far more than they are currently aware of."

"What are we supposed to do?"

Wikerus leaned back in his chair, his eyes on the Odd Squad. "Something you will not like one little bit, I'm afraid."

"What is it? What do we have to do? Is it really dangerous? Super scary?"

"You must wait, let the chain of events play out as it will. You will know exactly what to do when the time comes."

"We just sit around and wait? Do nothing?"

Wikerus smiled. "Remind me again of the inscription on your work ring?"

"Open your eyes and see."

"Precisely. While you are waiting, be aware of everything happening around you. Eyes open, vigilant."

Chapter 7

Texting

That evening, Odo kept a close watch on the sampler, texting the others each time there was a change.

There are four more people, and they're holding torches, not lanterns.

The ground is covered with snow.

There's a white dog, maybe a fox, standing next to the person by the house.

I think one of the torch people has a gun, a musket.

Two of the trees are burning.

They all met the following day at lunch, Silas plopping down in his chair, staring at his lunch tray. "Do you think this is meat?"

Odo studied it. "Hard to tell. It could be beans all

mashed together and cooked."

Silas poked at it with a fork. "Beans." He took a bite. "Not bad." He looked up at the others. "I have an idea, an absolutely stunningly brilliant one. Prepare to be amazed."

Odo groaned. "We're so doomed, Silas has been thinking again."

Sephie kicked Odo's foot. "What's your amazing idea?"

"Wait for it, wait for it…"

Odo gave an exasperated sigh. "Spill it, boy genius."

Silas laughed. "If we can see someone embroidering on the sampler, would they be able to see us if we embroidered something on it?"

The others looked at each other, Odo's jaw dropping. He clapped Silas on the back. "That is genius! We could talk to her, embroider words."

"Kind of like texting, only super slow."

"Does anyone know how to embroider?"

Emmy said, "My grandma showed me how when I was little. It's not that hard, but it's kind of tedious. I can make simple letters though."

"Do you think it will work? Do you think they'll see it?"

Silas shrugged. "Only one way to find out."

They stopped at the store on the way home, Emmy buying a packet of embroidering needles and some black thread.

As they strolled down Asper Street toward Odo's house, Silas said, "What should we say to them?"

Odo thought for a minute, then said, "How about something like, *Greetings from the twenty-first century. We are Odo, Sephie, Silas, and Emmy, and together, we are the Odd Squad. We were wondering if by any chance you were the one who was embroidering the–*"

Sephie punched his arm. "You're a lunatic."

Emmy said, "We could just say *Hello*."

"Do you think she'll freak out when she sees it? She lives in 1749 and doesn't know anything about temporal nonlocality or quantum physics."

"She'll just think it's magic."

"You're right, that works."

They darted up the front steps to Odo's house, running up to his room.

Emmy carefully threaded the embroidery needle. "I'm kind of nervous. She'll probably laugh at my bad embroidering."

Silas stared at her. "Seriously? That's what you're worried about?"

"I'm just not very good at it, that's all." She picked up the sampler, carefully embroidering the word *HELLO*. "What do you think? The letters are a little crooked, I could take it out and do that part again with the–"

"It's perfect. You're amazing."

"Now we wait. We don't know what time it is there, she might be sleeping."

"We don't even know if she'll be able to see it."

The four friends watched the sampler for almost an hour, Sephie finally saying, "I should get going, my mom is going to be home pretty soon."

"We should go, too."

Odo said, "I'll keep checking on it and text everyone if anything happens."

That evening at dinner, Odo's dad said, "Your tour of the university is on Saturday?"

"Sephie and I are both going."

"We need to talk about your tuition. We have some money set aside to help pay for it, but not enough for all of it."

"I've saved a bunch of money from my job at Serendipity Salvage. I have almost seven thousand dollars."

"That will help, but it's not nearly enough, college tuition is very expensive."

"I'm going to apply for scholarships. I have amazing grades and I've taken lots of advanced placement classes."

"We'll take it one step at a time. First you have to get accepted, then we find out about scholarships. We can get student loans if we have to."

"Why is everything so expensive?"

Petunia rubbed his shoulder. "We'll figure it out. I'm sure you'll get a scholarship, maybe one that pays all your tuition."

"That would be amazing. I should probably head

upstairs and study. I have a big test tomorrow."

Odo darted up the stairs to his room, stopping short when he glanced at the sampler on his desk, his eyes locked onto a single word embroidered in bright orange thread.

Angels?

He grabbed his phone, sending a picture of the sampler to the others.

What do you think this means?

She's asking if you're an angel

I know that, but what should I say?

Just say "friend"

Okay, I'll try to embroider it, not sure what it will look like

Odo hung up, sitting down at his desk. It took a minute, but he finally managed to thread the needle and began embroidering. "This is way harder than it looks. It's hard to stitch the round parts. Looks kind of weird, like a little kid wrote it."

Finally he had stitched the word *FRIEND*.

48

A few minutes later two words slowly appeared.

Help us?

Odo embroidered his reply.

How?

They come

Who?

Others. To kill us.

When?

Soon. I am Solis.

Odo sank back in his chair. What was happening here? Someone was coming to kill the girl? Who were the Others? They had to do something, but what? Odo grabbed his phone and texted Sephie, telling her what Solis had said.

Her name is Solis and she needs help, she says the Others are coming to kill them. She said they were coming soon. We have to help her.

Temporal shifting. You and I can go.

Use the sampler as a temporal waystone?

Bingo. I'll come to your house before school.

Okay, see you then.

Chapter 8

Solis

Odo was finishing his breakfast when he heard a knock on the front door.

Petunia said, "Who could that be?"

"It's Sephie. She's riding the bus with me. We're making a list of questions to ask on our college tour."

"Wonderful idea. I'm off to my study group at school. Have a great day."

Odo ran to the door, flinging it open. "Hey, Seph, I told my mom about us taking the bus so we could make a list of questions for tomorrow."

Sephie nodded. "Right, the list of questions."

Petunia headed out the door. "Don't be late for school."

"We won't. Bye!"

Sephie said, "Show me the sampler."

Odo pulled it from his backpack, setting it on the table.

Sephie stared at it. "It's changing, she's embroidering something."

Odo watched as the words formed.

Others here

Odo said, "We have to go."

"I know. We can temporal shift to 1749 using the sampler as a waystone, then return a few minutes from now at Wikerus' house using our homestones. We'll have plenty of time to catch the bus."

"But how are we going to talk to–"

"We have to leave. Now!"

Odo grabbed the sampler, taking Sephie's hand. "When I temporal shifted before, I was like a ghost, no one could see me. How will Solis see us?"

"I have a plan. Hurry!"

Odo pressed his hand against the sampler, imagining an old fashioned radio dial, turning it slowly in his mind until the frequencies of his physical form aligned with the deep temporal frequencies of the sampler. When they were perfectly in tune his body would turn solid, and they would shift back in time.

"That's it, my hands are turning–"

There was a brilliant flash of light, the two friends finding themselves standing in front of a small crudely constructed wooden house with a single window made from four small panes of rippling glass. He turned, his eyes on the shadowy forest, on the torches flickering through the trees.

"They're almost here, there's a bunch of them, who-ever they are."

Odo glanced at Sephie, her vaporous spectral form floating next to him. " Can the villagers see us?"

"Not now, but they're going to. I've been practicing something Elia taught me on Varania. I can create a vis-ible form while I'm using the Traveling Eye."

"We're not using that though, we're temporal shift-ing."

"It's kind of the same thing. Ready?"

"I guess so."

Odo felt a strange force rippling through him, his ghostly body becoming translucent, shimmering with light.

"Whoa, that's spooky looking."

"I'm counting on it. Let's go talk to Solis."

They floated toward the front door of the small house, Odo spotting a frightened face in the window, a teenage girl with white hair and green eyes. Sephie drifted through the front door, a startled old woman looking up at them, a teacup falling from her hand, shattering on the floor.

"You are angels? You have come to take us home?"

"We're not angels."

Solis said, "You are the ones who spoke to me through the sampler?"

Sephie eyed Solis' long handsewn linen dress, won-dering how anyone could run in clothes like that. "That's us. We are here to help you, but we're not angels. What do the people with torches want?"

"They are from the village of the Others, outside the forest. They think I am a forest witch because of my white hair and green eyes. They want to kill us. I don't wish to hurt them, but I'm afraid I might. I can't control it, I might do something I don't mean to do."

Sephie studied the girl's brain waves curiously.

Odo said, "How would you hurt them? You have weapons?"

The old woman answered. "She is born of angels, her powers coming from a distant heavenly realm."

Odo looked at Sephie. "What do you think?"

"I think it's showtime."

"You get to say it, but I don't?"

"You can say it if you want."

"It doesn't work like that. I have to say it first or it doesn't count. How do we make the villagers leave?"

"I'm going to implant some scary illusions in their minds."

"What kind of illusions?"

"How about a terrifying prehistoric spinosaurus running toward them? Nothing scarier than a giant spinosaurus."

"Except for two giant spinosauruses."

Sephie laughed, floating through the front door, her eyes on the gathering crowd of villagers waving their flaming torches.

"Why are they dressed like it's winter? It's summertime."

"I have no idea."

The villagers cried out in fear at the sight of the two shimmering translucent figures emerging from the house, some of them raising their muskets in the air.

"Demons from the underworld! Burn them all!"

Odo looked at Sephie with a grin. "You know, when the light hits you just the right way, you do look a lot like a demon from the underworld."

"Thanks, Odo. Okay, here we go." She closed her eyes, sending a powerful wave of thought toward the villagers. They screamed when they saw the monstrous roaring prehistoric spinosaurus lumbering toward them. Twenty-seconds later they were gone.

Sephie laughed. "That was easy, and no one got hurt."

Odo said, "Solis is kind of different looking. I like her green eyes though, really cool."

Sephie gave Odo a look he hadn't seen since the time she told him about the popular girl at school who thought he was cute and wanted to go out with him.

Odo froze. "I mean, cool in a spooky sort of way. You know, weird, eerie, almost creepy, if I think about it."

"She has green eyes and white hair because she's an alien. She has powers that she doesn't understand, and can't control. Wikerus said she doesn't know how powerful she is."

"We scared away the Others, but won't they just keep

coming back? We can't always be here to protect them."

"You're right, and I have an idea, but we have to talk to Solis and her mom about it."

"You're going to teach her how to control her powers?"

"That would take too long. I want to do something else, I want to bring Solis back to Bedford Falls with us."

Chapter 9

The New World

Sephie and Odo floated back into the house, drifting over to Solis and her mom. "The villagers are gone for now. We scared them away, but I'm afraid they'll come back with more people, more torches, and more guns. We can't always be here to protect you from them."

Solis turned to her mom. "What can we do? Should we leave the forest? Find another cabin?"

Her mom shook her head. "No, dear one. In this world, there will always be villagers who are afraid of things they do not comprehend. When the angel came down from the heavens and brought you to me, he told me that one day you would have to leave. I have long dreaded that day, but I see clearly now that it is meant to be. You must return to the world of angels, you must fulfill your destiny."

Sephie said, "What did the angel look like?"

"It was solid in form and white as the driven snow, floating effortlessly above the ground. I could not see its face, but the angel's presence filled me with a joy I had never known."

Odo glanced at Sephie.

Solis took her mother's hand in hers. "I can't leave you here. It's too dangerous. I will stay with you. I will use my angel powers to protect us if I have to."

"My sister has told me many times that I am welcome to live with her if I ever choose to do so. I believe I have coins enough for passage to her village."

Sephie thought for a moment, then said, "Would you mind showing me the coins? I'd like to try something."

Solis gave her a puzzled look, but ran to a cupboard, returning with a small brass box. She opened it, setting it down in front of Sephie. There were three silver coins, nine copper coins, and one small gold coin.

Sephie eyed the gold coin, studying it closely. "I've never done this before, but it might work." She closed her eyes, her shimmering body slowly gaining substance and form until she was solid. "I can't stay in this form for very long."

She picked up the gold coin, turning it over her hand, visualizing it in her mind until it was sharp and clear, a powerful swirling thought cloud appearing above the table. She spoke to her deeper self, asking it to compress the thought cloud into physical matter. Seconds later, dozens of gold coins tumbled down onto the table. Sephie's body faded back to the shimmering blue spectral form.

Odo said, "How did you make yourself solid?"

Sephie didn't answer, turning to Solis and her mom. "These coins are for you."

Solis' mom stared at the pile of gleaming gold coins. "You are an angel, sent from the heavens above. My sister and I shall never want for anything again."

"We're not angels, we're just people."

Solis' mother put her arms around Solis, then said, "It is a truth known to all that a time shall come when every child must go forth and seek their fortune. That day has come for you, dear one. I shall be content living with my sister, knowing that you are in the company of angels, back in the heavenly realm that is your true home."

"I won't go, I can't leave you."

Sephie said, "We can bring you back to visit your mom whenever you want."

"This is true?"

"It is true, I promise."

"Go with them, and visit me when you are able."

"Very well, I will go." Solis gave her mom a long hug. "You will stay safe, leave the forest soon? You must promise me."

"I will leave at sunrise. The forest was never my home, but it was our safe haven until the villagers found us. Before you leave, there is something I must give you." She disappeared into her room, returning with a small crystal box. Opening it, she removed a glowing medallion on a silver chain. "The angel said that one day you would need this."

Solis took the medallion, carefully putting it around her neck. "I will visit you, I promise."

Sephie said, "We should go."

"How do we travel to your world?"

"First we have to hold hands." Sephie took Solis' hand, then Odo's.

Solis' eyes were on her mother. "I love you."

"And I love you, dear one."

"I'm ready."

Odo gripped his homestone. "Here we go." He visualized the radio dial in his mind, aligning his deeper vibrations to those of his homestone. It didn't take long, the three friends vanishing in a blink of light, appearing a moment later in Wikerus Praevian's sitting room, the origin point of Odo's homestone.

A startled Wikerus Praevian looked up from his book, his eyes on the friends. "Good heavens, this is a surprise."

Odo grinned. "We finally managed to surprise you?"

"You have indeed." He studied Solis for a moment, then called out, "Mrs. Preke, I am going to need your help."

Mrs. Preke appeared in a flash of light, Solis skittering back in surprise, the room suddenly icy cold, Odo shivering.

Mrs. Preke gave Solis a warm smile. "I'm sorry, dear, I didn't mean to startle you. You're safe here. We'll take care of you, nothing to worry about. You are among friends."

There was something about the tone of Mrs. Preke's voice that gave great comfort to Solis, her fear vanishing, the room warm again.

Mrs. Preke smiled. "That's a lovely medallion you're wearing. Was it a gift from your mother?"

"It was a gift from the angels."

"I see, very lovely indeed."

Odo's eyes narrowed. Why was Mrs. Preke so interested in the medallion?

Solis' voice was low, almost reverent. "Am I in the realm of angels?"

Mrs. Preke shook her head. "No, we are not angels, but we do need to have a lovely long chat and get to know each other. I will answer all your questions, tell you everything you want to know about this world." She turned to Odo and Sephie. "You two run off to school while I visit with Solis."

Sephie gave Solis a quick hug. "It will be okay. It won't take long for you to get used to this world, I promise." She hesitated, studying Solis' long linen dress. "I'll bring you some new clothes so you won't look out of place here. We could both go and get our hair done too. Yours is kind of long, and mine is getting a little wild looking."

"My hair is too long? They will think me a forest witch?"

"No one will think you're a witch here, but it is a little

bit old fashioned looking."

Wikerus flicked his hand, a box of chocolates appearing on the table. "Chocolates, anyone? They're quite delicious."

Solis' eyes widened, her eyes on the box of chocolates. She turned to Wikerus. "I have never met a wizard before."

"Oh, it's nothing like that. It's not magic, I'm afraid, just a little trick I learned."

"What are chocolates?"

Sephie said, "You're going to love them, I promise. We have to go, we'll see you after school."

Odo grabbed two chocolates from the box. "The orange creams are the best. So good."

The friends headed outside, walking briskly down the sidewalk, arriving at the bus stop just as the bus rounded the corner and rattled to a stop, the doors squealing open.

They scrambled up the steps, Odo flopping down on the seat next to Sephie, saying, "Why did it get so cold when Mrs. Preke got there? Did Solis do that?"

"I think it frightened Solis when Mrs. Preke appeared in a flash of light, and she unconsciously made it cold. She said she did the same thing to the villagers the first time they showed up. She froze everything around her. That's why the ground was covered in snow on her sampler."

"How does she do it?"

"I don't know, and I don't think she knows either. She

has a power, but she doesn't understand it or know how to control it. It scares her, like my powers used to scare me when I didn't understand them."

"I wonder what else she can do? Wikerus said she was really powerful. Making stuff cold is sort of a cool power, I guess. If the electricity went out and the food in your freezer was melting, you could freeze it."

Sephie stared at him. "What?"

"I'm just saying, making stuff cold is okay, but it doesn't seem like a very useful power."

"Suppose you were being chased by a spinosaurus and you came to a wide river filled with thousands of deadly snapping piranha. What would you do?"

"First of all, that would never happen because piranha didn't exist in the same time period as–"

"What would you do?"

"I'd say something nice to the spinosaurus, maybe compliment him on his big shiny teeth, make friends with him, ingratiate myself."

"Solis could freeze the river and you could cross over, but the ice wouldn't hold the weight of the spinosaurus."

"I never thought of that. Do you think she absorbs thermal energy from her surroundings? Is that how it works?"

"That would make sense. I wonder how much energy she can absorb?"

"I just thought of something, she could keep the ice cream from melting on the way back from the grocery store if you had other shopping to do."

Sephie punched his arm. "You're such a maroon."

"Are you ready for our tour of Pravus University tomorrow? They'll probably give us both full scholarships."

"Dream on. Wear some nice clothes and don't make any dumb jokes on the tour."

"That won't be a problem since I don't know any dumb jokes."

Sephie snorted. "Wear nice clothes."

Chapter 10

Professor Beauvais

The following day Odo and Sephie climbed aboard the city bus, heading off to Pravus University.

Sephie said, "You're solid, you decided to wear your Sinarian ring?"

"I thought it would make things a little easier if they could see me."

"Good idea."

When Odo and Sephie had returned from their adventures on Atroxia, a Sinarian had given each of them a ring; Odo's ring made him solid, and Sephie's ring made her translucent.

"You texted Silas and Emmy, told them we brought Solis back with us?"

"I did. They can't wait to meet her. I said she was really nice."

"Mrs. Preke seemed really interested in her medallion."

"Do you remember how Solis' mom described the angel?"

"I do, and it sounded like she was describing a Sinarian; no face, floating above the ground, pure white, communicating with thoughts."

"Exactly. Solis' medallion was given to her by a Sinarian, not an angel."

"And they were the ones who brought her to the forest when she was little."

"And that's why Mrs. Preke was so interested in the medallion."

"We know Solis was about two years old when the Sinarian left her in the forest, but we don't know where she came from, or why the Sinarian wanted Solis' mom to take care of her."

"They were protecting her from something, hiding her. Maybe they rescued her from a war, or maybe some crazy emperor found out about her powers, was afraid of her, and sent an assassin to kill her, but the Sinarians jumped in and saved her at the last second."

"Right. Whatever it was, the Sinarians went to a lot of trouble to hide her in the forest. I wish I knew where she was from, or when she was from. They could have brought her back in time to 1749. She might be from a future high tech alien civilization."

"Advanced high tech civilizations like that have been around for hundreds of millions of years. She could be from the past, hundreds of thousands of years ago, and they brought her to the future."

"True."

Odo looked up when the bus shuddered to a halt, the driver calling out, "Pravus University!"

The two friends jumped up, hopping off the bus. Sephie eyed the bustling campus. "Which way?"

Odo checked his notes. "We're supposed to meet our guide at a big statue in front of the Old North building. She said the building was built in 1794."

"The school is that old?"

"I guess so. Look, down there, a big statue of a guy sitting in a chair. That must be it."

"He's probably one of the university founders."

They headed across the sprawling manicured lawn, past groups of students sitting on the grass talking and reading.

"That will be us next year."

When they reached the statue, Odo looked around for their guide. "She said she has red hair."

"Over there, that must be her." They stepped over to a girl standing near the statue. "Are you Peyton?"

She turned, giving them a bright smile. "I am, and that means you must be Odo and Sephie. Welcome to Pravus University."

"Thanks, it's a lot bigger than we thought it would be."

"It is pretty big, and very old. You're thinking about applying here?"

"I'm interested in engineering, and Odo is interested in physics."

"Wonderful, this is the place to go for physics and engineering. I'll take you over to the Reiss Science Center and we can visit the engineering and physics departments. They have a big research center there, it's quite well known." She leaned toward them, whispering, "Lots of secret stuff going on there."

Odo said, "What kind of secret stuff?"

Peyton shook her head, laughing. "I don't really know, I'm a music major, but I've heard rumors. It's probably secret government research or something."

"That sounds interesting."

They strolled across the campus to the science center, heading up the steps and through the main doors.

"Lots of the undergraduate classes are taught in this wing of the science center. There are no classes today so we can check out some of the lecture halls and the labs."

They headed down a long corridor, peering through windows at the science labs, Odo recognizing a lot of the equipment. He grinned to himself. This was primitive compared to the tech they had seen on other worlds.

A door swung open down the hall, a man with long white hair and a white beard stepping out, heading in their direction.

Peyton whispered, "That's Professor Beauvais. Some of the students call him Professor Santa."

Odo laughed. "I can see why."

The professor glanced at them, then stopped abruptly, his eyes on Odo and Sephie.

Peyton said, "Hello, Professor. I'm giving Odo and Sephie a tour of the science center. They're thinking about applying to the university, majoring in engineering and physics."

The professor approached them, nodding, his eyes on Sephie's orange hair. "You're interested in physics, are you?"

Sephie nodded. "Engineering for me, and physics for Odo." As she spoke to him she was scanning the professor's brainwaves. His hypothalamus was flaring brightly. That was curious.

The professor stroked his white beard. "I have no pressing engagements at the moment. Perhaps you two would like a personally guided tour of the research center? I think you'll find it most interesting."

"Really? That would be amazing."

Peyton smiled, saying, "I'll leave you with the professor, then. It was nice meeting you both. Enjoy your tour, guys."

"Thanks."

Odo and Sephie followed Professor Beauvais down the hall to two windowless silver doors. He pressed his hand against a dark gray rectangle on the wall, saying, "Professor Beauvais, plus two." The doors hissed open.

"This way, if you would." They stepped into a long corridor, walking past a guard smartly dressed in a jet black uniform. Odo's eyes widened when he saw the patch on his arm. He nudged Sephie. She nodded.

The professor said, "There's a great deal of extremely valuable equipment here which must be guarded around the clock." He pointed to a long glass window running along the corridor. "Our current project, over ten years in the making. There's nothing else like it in the world. Would you like to see it?"

Odo was getting an oddly uncomfortable feeling. There was something off about the professor. "We're just thinking about applying to Pravus, we don't really know anything about all the—"

"I like your ring." The professor smiled, pointing to Odo's hand.

"My ring?"

"It's unique, I've never seen one like it."

"Um, thanks, my dad gave it to me."

"How nice. Follow me, if you would." He pressed his hand against another dark gray panel. "Professor Beauvais, plus two." The door hissed open, Odo and Sephie following the professor into a brightly lit room.

Odo scanned the room, his eyes coming to rest on the long bank of massive supercomputers, thousands of small blinking yellow and green lights.

Professor Beauvais said, "Quantum computers. We've had them for almost five years now."

"You've had quantum computers for five years? Really?"

The professor gave Odo a cryptic smile.

Sephie eyed a ten-foot wide black display panel at the

far end of the room. "What is all this for? What does it do?"

"This way." Professor Beauvais stepped through an array of electronic equipment, stopping at a long curved control console in front of the enormous black screen.

Odo glanced at Sephie. She was looking just as confused as he was.

The professor studied the control center, absently picking up a blue crystal sphere, rolling it back and forth in his hands. "Ahh, there it is. Would you mind holding this for a moment? Don't drop it." He handed the sphere to Sephie, picking up a small black rectangular device with six glowing buttons on it.

Sephie said, "Why are you showing this to us?"

The professor gave them a distracted smile. "One moment."

Odo glanced at Sephie. There was something really off about the professor. He watched as Professor Beauvais tapped four of the buttons on the black device, the wide display panel shimmering with an eerie blue light.

"What is it doing?"

Professor Beauvais didn't answer, pressing a series of glowing tabs on the main control panel. A wavering image began to appear on the screen, seconds later becoming sharp and clear. Sephie froze when she saw it, her heart pounding. This was not good, not good at all. They had to get out of here, now. She turned away from the professor, sending out a powerful thought to the XODC guard.

The professor looked at her. "Marvelous, isn't it?"

Sephie nodded, doing her best to look puzzled.

Odo said, "What is that?"

There was a sudden frenetic rapping on the glass window, a guard in a black uniform motioning for the professor to come out. Professor Beauvais stepped over to the door, opening it, the guard whispering something in his ear.

The professor turned to Odo and Sephie, an annoyed look on his face. "Unfortunately I am being called away on some rather urgent business. Do let me know when you apply to the university. I'll make certain both of you receive full scholarships to the school of your choice. Leave your contact information with the main office."

Odo gaped at him. "What?"

The guard rapped on the window again, the doors sliding open.

Twenty minutes later Odo and Sephie were riding home on the bus.

"What just happened? What was that? Why did he say we'd get full scholarships? Why didn't you want to leave our contact information at the main office?"

Sephie looked at Odo, her face pale. "This is bad, Odo. We're in trouble. Big, big trouble."

Chapter 11

Solis 2.0

"What could possibly be bad about both of us getting full scholarships at Pravus?"

"He knows, Odo. He knows what we are."

"What do you mean?"

"You didn't recognize the image on the screen?"

"Not really, it was just a big city."

"It's not just a big city. I've seen it before, Wikerus showed me pictures of it. It's the capital city of Fortisia."

"Fortisia? How is that possible? Why would he have a picture of that?"

"It was a live image, vehicles were moving."

Odo furrowed his brow. "He made you hold that blue crystal sphere. Do you think it was scanning you?"

"The machine knew where I was from. They have a device that detects aliens and can tell where they're from. I don't trust him at all, and I knew we had to get out of there. I implanted a memory in the guard, a vitally important meeting the professor had forgotten."

"Good one. He asked about my Sinarian ring, said it

was unique. That was weird. Maybe he knows about the Sinarians."

"The guard in the black uniform had an XODC patch on his sleeve."

"I saw that, Exo Defense Command, the secret branch of the military that's supposed to be protecting Earth from aliens. Mrs. Bailey told us about them. She was a Fortisian and she did not like the XODC at all."

"I was scanning the professor's brain waves, and he was totally up to something."

Odo said, "This is kind of scary. Could you wipe his memory? Make him forget he met us?"

"I could, but the guard saw us, and the lab is full of security cameras recording everything. It wouldn't take them long to realize I'd erased his memory, and that would make things a lot worse."

"Maybe it's not so bad, maybe they want people like us at the school. That project looked really interesting. The quantum computers they have were amazing. It was pretty cool."

"I scanned his brainwaves and he's not jolly old Professor Santa. He's up to something, and it's not good. Not good at all."

"We should tell Wikerus that Professor Beauvais knows you're Fortisian and he might know about the Sinarians."

"Good idea, let's go see him. We can check on Solis, see how she's doing."

"Suppose the professor has XODC agents watching us? If they see us go into Wikerus' house, they'll want to know who lives there, and why we're visiting him."

"Take off your ring so you're translucent." Sephie reached into her coat pocket, pulling out her Sinarian ring, slipping it onto her finger. "Problem solved, we're both translucent."

"You carry your Sinarian ring with you?"

"You never know."

"Smart. Okay, let's go see Wikerus."

They hopped off the bus, heading down Expergo Avenue to Wikerus' house, knocking on the door.

Seconds later it swung open, Mrs. Preke looking at them curiously. "Why are you both translucent?"

"The XODC might be following us. A professor at Pravus University knows I'm Fortisian."

Odo said, "They have a machine there that detects aliens and can tell where they're from."

"I see. We'll need to tell Wikerus."

They headed down the hallway into the sitting room. Wikerus was seated in his chair, Solis sitting on the blue embroidered couch reading a book. She jumped up when she saw Odo and Sephie.

Sephie's jaw dropped with she saw Solis. "What happened? You look amazing!"

Mrs. Preke said, "I researched online trending fashions and updated Solis' appearance. What do you think?"

Odo said, "You look fantastic, like a supermodel."

Sephie glanced at Odo, then said, "You do look fantastic."

"It feels so strange to have short hair." She leaned forward, whispering, "It's so embarrassing to be wearing men's trousers instead of a dress. People will stare and laugh."

"Those are called jeans. Everyone wears them, men and women. No one will laugh at you, I promise. You look amazing."

"My shoes are so light I can scarcely feel them, but they're so soft and comfortable. Have you tried the chocolates? I can't stop eating them. They're heavenly."

Odo nodded. "They're so good. I love the orange creams. And the lemon creams."

Mrs. Preke said, "Solis is quite an astonishing young lady. She's been through over a dozen history books in the short time she's been here."

Solis said, "It was confusing at first, but I have a better understanding of your world now, and it no longer seems magical to me. I read much about the scientific discoveries and advancements in technology made since 1749. Do you think I could ride on an airplane?"

Sephie laughed. "Maybe ride in a car first, see how you like it." She turned to Wikerus, her smile fading. "We're here because a professor at Pravus University knows I'm a Fortisian. They have a machine that can identify someone's world of origin."

"What did the professor say to you?"

"He said he would make sure we both get full scholarships to Pravus. "

"Tell me about this machine he has."

Sephie and Odo described in great detail the huge lab with its quantum computers and enormous black display panel.

"When Sephie held the blue glass sphere, an image of Fortisia showed up on the screen."

"You're certain it was just an image, nothing more?"

"What do you mean?"

"It's quite possible you were looking through a portal to Fortisia, that it wasn't simply an image on a screen."

"They have an interstellar portal there? Really?"

"XODC has managed to obtain a certain amount of found alien technology, quantum computing and simple interstellar portals being two of them."

"So it's not a big deal that they know about Sephie?"

Wikerus hesitated. "It's not so much what the professor knows now, but what he might come to know in the future."

"Like what?"

Wikerus didn't answer. "During your absence I created a new identity for Solis, entering her personal history into the national database systems."

"So if anyone does a background check on her, she'll be okay?"

"I was very thorough. She's safe here for now. She will stay with us until we understand the deeper purpose of her visit."

Odo said, "We know the Sinarians brought her to the forest in about 1735, when she was two years old, but we don't know where she's from."

Wikerus nodded. "It is a puzzle, indeed."

"You don't know where she's from?"

"There are many things in this world that I do not know, and that is one of them."

Solis said, "I told Mrs. Preke and Wikerus about my angel powers."

Mrs. Preke nodded. "We are not currently aware of any world where the inhabitants are able to manipulate thermal energy on a scale such as that."

"What do you mean, on a scale such as that?"

"All we know for certain is that Solis is an astonishingly powerful being, and that is why we have to keep her safe."

"Do you think that's why the Sinarians hid her?"

"More than likely they knew how powerful she would become, and what would happen if such power fell into the wrong hands."

"Like Professor Beauvais?"

Wikerus nodded. "Like Professor Beauvais and the XODC."

Chapter 12

A Surprise Visit

Solis woke up the next morning with a nagging sensation that wouldn't leave her. A feeling of expectation, as if she was waiting for something to happen that she already knew was going to happen, but she couldn't remember what it was. She had no idea what she was waiting for, but she knew it was something that would bring her joy. She hopped out of bed, pulling on her clothes.

"I can't imagine what it could be. I've never had a feeling like this before. Maybe Sephie and Odo are coming to see me today. They've been so nice to me."

She stood in front of the mirror, gazing at her reflection. "I don't believe I shall ever get used to wearing these jean pants. It's so peculiar to see myself in them, dressed like a man, but everyone wears them here, and no one makes fun of the girls who do."

She took a seat at a lustrous mahogany desk, leaning back in a padded swivel chair.

"It's so confusing. The Sinarian told my mother it was my destiny to leave the forest, that I was to become a savior. If I can't even wear jean pants without being embarrassed, how am I supposed to be a savior? Odo and Sephie and their friends have shown me nothing but kindness, but still, I do not feel a part of this world. I wish I did not feel so alone. I miss the silence of the forest, and I miss my dearest friend Fox. How I wish he could be with me now. He would know exactly what to say."

She turned when she heard a scratching noise behind her, giving a yelp when she saw the source of the sound.

"FOX!"

Fox tilted his head, his eyes on Solis.

A jumble of thoughts poured out of her. *"Is it really you? How can it be? I saw you die, the villager shot you with his musket. Where did you go? Where have you been?"*

"I did not go anywhere. My death was an illusion, one designed to cause the overwhelming grief and anger necessary to awaken your powers. Birth of any kind is painful and chaotic, and this was no exception."

"You gave me my powers? Are you an angel who has taken the form of a fox?"

"Your powers are your powers, and I am a fox, there is no need to call either by any other name."

"But you died, I saw you. And now you are alive. It's a miracle."

"It was not true death, it was an illusion, a trick. Often times painful, unwanted events bring about near miraculous transformations. You are destined to become a

great savior, but you needed to awaken your hidden pow-ers. You have always known you were meant for more than life in the forest."

"It is true, the forest was my home, but it was also not my home. I felt lost, as though in a dream, homesick for a world I knew existed, but one I could not describe or even remember."

"Always pay close attention to such feelings, as they are never wrong, even if they contradict your most logi-cal of assumptions."

"How can a fox know such things as you do?"

"The day will come when you will understand. I will tell you this much; with the help of your new friends, Odo, Sephie, Silas, and Emmy, you will soon return to your true home to confront great chaos and overwhelm-ing obstacles. You will need your powers to survive, but first you must learn to control them. Seek help from your new friends. I will guide you when I can. I must leave you now."

"Wait, don't–"

Solis watched as Fox faded away to nothingness.

* * * *

The Odd Squad met up in the school cafeteria, Emmy and Silas asking a stream of questions about Solis.

"What's she like? Was she freaked out by all the mod-ern technology? Will she go to school here?"

"It was a shock for her at first, but she's really interested in our technology and how the world has changed since 1749. She wants to know how everything works, like cars and airplanes, and my phone. She loves my phone. We made sure she knows our technology is not the work of angels. She also knows it wasn't an angel who brought her to the forest. We told her it was a Sinarian, a highly advanced living being."

Odo blurted out, "Mrs. Preke gave her a makeover. She looks like a supermodel."

Silas grinned. "Really? A supermodel?"

Emmy looked at Silas. "What's with the goofy grin?"

"What? Nothing, I was just... you know... it's kind of funny... that she would look like a supermodel?"

"Hilarious."

Sephie said, "Wikerus wants her to stay hidden for now. He's afraid Professor Beauvais and the XODC might be watching us, and he doesn't want them to find out about Solis."

"What about that portal you saw at the university? Do you know what they're using it for?"

Odo said, "All we know for certain is the professor used a blue crystal sphere to scan Sephie, then created a portal to Fortisia, her world of origin. The machine knew where she was from."

"That's scary. What's even scarier is if they open a portal to some weird world and accidentally let crazy creatures come through. I don't think the XODC has any idea what's out there, how dangerous that portal could be."

"Wikerus doesn't know where Solis is from?"

"No, but it must be a world where the people have amazing powers."

Silas set his fork down, looking at Odo. "Wait, what about Professor Beauvais' portal machine?"

"Hello, Earth to Silas, we just told you all about the portal machine. Professor Beauvais had a blue crystal sphere that he gave to Sephie so he could–"

"I know all that, but couldn't we use the portal machine to find out where Solis is from?"

Odo blinked. "That's brilliant! You are so much smarter than you look."

Emmy laughed.

"How would we get in there to use it? The lab is totally secure, guarded by the XODC, cameras everywhere."

Odo studiously rubbed his chin. "Hmm… if only we knew someone who was translucent and could walk through walls."

"Oh, right. We could sneak in at night. The professor said it's guarded around the clock, but Sephie could take care of the guards, no problem."

"I can make them fall asleep, or implant false memories so they'll leave the lab."

Emmy said, "Once we're in there and the guards are gone, what do we do? Do you guys know how to operate the portal machine?"

Odo answered, "I was sort of watching the professor when he used it. He had some kind of black remote thing with lights and then he hit a bunch of buttons on a big curved control panel."

Silas snorted. "What could possibly go wrong?"

"Excuse me, I was a little busy wondering if the crazy professor was going to lock us up in some weird prison?"

Sephie said, "I know what we can do."

"Wait, couldn't we just download the owner's manual from the XODC website?" Odo gave a crazy laugh, slapping his leg.

Emmy snickered.

"Two words, Traveling Eye. I'll go in and watch the professor use the machine, see exactly what he does."

"That's perfect, no one will be able to see you."

Emmy continued, "So let's say we get in there and we find out where Solis is from, what do we do then?"

"It's a portal, so she could go home, back to her world."

"A world she knows nothing about?"

Silas frowned. "Emmy is right, it could be a violent post apocalyptic world, or there might be people there who want to harm her. There's a reason why the Sinarians took her from that world. She must have been in danger. We can't send her back to a world like that."

"We need to learn more about her world, and we need to go with her."

"The first step is learning how to operate the portal."

"What about her medallion? Wouldn't that be from her world? We could use it as a waystone."

"Except we don't know what the medallion is, what it does, or where it came from. A Sinarian gave it to her, but that's all we know. It could be from Sinaria, or it could be alien tech from any one of a million other worlds."

The lunch bell rang, Sephie grabbing her books. "I'll use the Traveling Eye when I get home and visit the portal room. Hopefully Professor Beauvais will be there and I can watch him operate it."

"And maybe find out what they're using it for. Whatever it is, it's probably not good."

Chapter 13

The Wrong Guy

When she got home from school, Sephie ran up to her room, setting her backpack on the floor. She lay down on her bed, taking a deep breath, letting it out slowly.

Relaxing, she closed her eyes, letting go of her physical body, her consciousness drifting up above her bed. She looked down at her body, studying it. "I need a haircut. Maybe I should have Mrs. Preke give me a makeover like she gave Solis." She was remembering Odo's comment about Solis looking like a supermodel. It had bothered her a little, knowing that she would never look like Solis, never look like a supermodel, but she also knew deep down that she and Odo were connected, that Odo loved her. Even though he hadn't told her yet.

"Enough of that, it's time to go find out what Professor Beauvais is up to."

She shot up through the roof into the bright blue sky, turning slowly. "There it is, the university clock tower."

Sephie flashed across Bedford Falls, arriving at the college seconds later, flying toward the Reiss Science

Center.

"And in we go." She drifted through the front doors and down the hall to the heavily armored lab doors, floating into the portal room with its banks of jet black quantum computers. Professor Beauvais was hunched over the main control panel.

"My lucky day. Let's see what you're up to, jolly old Professor Santa."

She turned when she noticed two XODC guards coming down the hall, ushering a portly middle-aged man dressed in a rumpled tweed suit. Sephie froze. The man in the tweed suit was wearing handcuffs. Who was he? Why was he a prisoner here?

The doors slid open, the guards bringing in their visibly shaken captive.

"I don't know who you are, or what you want, but you have the wrong guy. Whatever you think I did, I didn't do it. I sell used cars, that's all I do. If you let me go I promise I won't say anything to anyone."

Professor Beauvais gave him a cold smile, a smile that sent a dreadful chill through Sephie. She did not like the feeling at all.

The professor shrugged. "We'll find out soon enough who you are and where you're from. Either way, you're not leaving this facility."

"Are you nuts? My name is Bob, I sell cars, that's all I–"

The professor picked up the blue crystal sphere,

stuffing it into the man's coat pocket, then reached over and grabbed the black remote from the console.

Sephie watched closely as one by one, four buttons lit up on the remote, each displaying a unique symbol. When the professor pressed them in the order they had appeared, the main control panel blinked on. He seemed almost cheerful, humming to himself as he studied the bank of blinking buttons on the console, one by one pressing the same four symbols that had appeared on the remote.

He stood back, his eyes on the immense portal, now shimmering with an eerie light, the image of a dark watery world appearing, a world with three moons.

The man in the tweed suit gave a start, a look of terror crossing his face, his eyes fixed on the portal image. "What is that? What are you doing?" The man glanced anxiously at the guards, then back to the professor.

The professor gave a thin smile. "Look familiar? Anything else you'd like to tell us, Bob?"

Everything changed in an instant, the man in the tweed suit replaced by a ferocious scaly creature bearing a strong resemblance to a humanoid crocodile. It snapped the metal handcuffs like they were made of paper, knocking one of the guards over, leaping toward the portal, the second guard firing a brilliant blue beam of light at the creature.

The crocodile man sank slowly to the ground, the professor watching, clearly amused.

"A valiant effort, my scaly alien friend, but not quite valiant enough. Take him back to his cell, we'll question him later, find out what he's doing here, run some tests on him. There's nothing lower than a slithering formshifter."

Sephie felt a dark anger rising up inside her. The crocodile man was a formshifter from another world, just like Wikerus and Mrs. Preke. It was clear to her now why their old friend Mrs. Bailey had detested the XODC. One thing she knew for certain, there was no way she and Odo would ever go to Pravus University, not if they were holding aliens prisoner, using them for experiments. The good news was, she had learned how to operate the portal.

Less than a minute later she was back in her room, eyes open. She jumped up and grabbed her phone from the table, texting Odo.

I know how to operate it. Bad things are happening there. I don't want to text it, I'll tell you tomorrow.

Okay, see you tomorrow.

When Odo hopped off the school bus the next day, Sephie was there waiting for him.

Odo said, "What did you see? What happened there?"

Sephie moved closer to him, whispering, "They're holding an alien prisoner there, maybe more than one.

The one I saw was a formshifter like Wikerus. He tried to jump through the portal but they stunned him with a beam weapon."

"They have an alien there? What was he like?"

"He was dressed in a tweed suit and told them he was a used car salesman, but when he saw his world through the portal, he formshifted back into a humanoid crocodile. He was really scared. The professor said they were going to run tests on him, told him he would never leave the lab."

Odo frowned. "They're going to run tests on him? What kind of tests?"

"I don't know, but it's not good, whatever it is. The worst thing was the professor seemed to be enjoying it. He thought it was funny."

"No way are we going to school there. We need to do something about Professor Beauvais."

"My thoughts exactly. We'll tell Emmy and Silas, then talk to Wikerus. Maybe he's learned something about Solis' world, where she's from."

"I know she was only two years old when they brought her here, but do you think she might remember anything at all about her world?"

"We can ask her. "

"Maybe Wikerus could hypnotize her or something."

After school the friends went to see Wikerus, telling him about the alien formshifter being held prisoner in the secret lab at Pravus University, and about Professor

Beauvais' plans to run tests on him.

Wikerus leaned back in his chair, eyeing Mrs. Preke. "What are your thoughts on the matter, Mrs. Preke?"

"My thoughts are that the formshifter must be returned to his home world through the portal, and Professor Beauvais' portal needs to be permanently closed."

Odo turned to Solis, saying, "Can you remember anything at all about your world? We know how to get you there now, but we don't know what your world is like, if it's dangerous."

Solis was silent for a moment, then said, "I can't remember anything, and I've tried so many times to see it, to imagine it, to remember it. There is something I must tell you that might help. Something happened this morning. It's going to seem quite strange, even to you."

All eyes were on Solis. "What do you mean, strange?"

"It will be simpler if I show you." She closed her eyes, sending out a thought.

"Fox, I need you."

Odo gave a start when the white fox appeared next to Solis, its bright green eyes fixed on the Odd Squad. "What is that?"

Silas nudged Odo. "It looks a lot like a white fox."

"Very funny."

"This is Fox. I met him in the forest when I was small. He's my dearest friend and trusted companion, but he's not a normal fox. I can talk to him with my thoughts. When the villagers shot him, I thought he was dead, but while I was holding him, his body vanished, faded away. He was gone. This morning he came back."

The four friends looked at each other, then at Fox.

"Is he a formshifter?"

"He's a fox."

"Right. What do you talk to him about?"

"We talk about everything, he's my dearest friend."

Emmy said, "You talk to him using your thoughts?"

Solis nodded. "I do, but I'm the only one who can hear him."

"Do you think Fox would know anything about your world?"

"That's what I wanted to tell you. Fox said my four new friends would be taking me home soon. He said we would confront great chaos and overwhelming obstacles. He said I would need my powers for us to survive, but I had to learn how to control them before we go. He told me to seek help from you."

Odo frowned. He didn't like the sound of great chaos and overwhelming obstacles.

Chapter 14

The Candle

Wikerus rose up from his chair, turning to Sephie. "Would you be willing to teach Solis how to use and control her powers?"

"What exactly are her powers?"

Wikerus didn't answer, stepping over to a tall mahogany highboy, pulling out a handful of white candles and a box of wooden matches.

"Solis is able to manipulate thermal energy, to absorb it and to project it. Start small, using these candles. You can practice in the drawing room."

Silas and Emmy stood up, grabbing their packs. "We have to go, but we'll see you guys tomorrow. Solis, did Fox tell you when we were taking you back to your world?"

She shook her head. "He just said it would be soon."

After Silas and Emmy left, Sephie, Odo, and Solis stepped into the drawing room, Odo eyeing the paintings on the wall. "This place looks like an art museum. What are we supposed to do with the candles?"

Solis said, "When the villagers arrived, they had torches. After they shot Fox, I made the torches go out and I froze everything, but I don't know how I did it."

"The trees burst into flames after you did that?"

Solis nodded.

Sephie picked up a brass candelabra. "Wikerus said you are able to absorb thermal energy from your surroundings, then project the energy back out again in concentrated form. That's how the trees caught fire."

Sephie placed four candles in a brass candelabra and set it on a table, lighting one of the candles.

"We'll start with something small. Try to absorb the heat from the candle flame, but nothing else, just the candle flame, and make it go out like the torches did."

Solis looked at Sephie, then at the flickering candle. "When it first happened I was really angry about them shooting Fox."

"You can do it without being angry. That's how powers work. The first time they appear is almost always when you're experiencing powerful, overwhelming emotions, when you're really angry or sad or scared."

"That makes sense. Fox said his death was a painful illusion designed to awaken my powers." Solis stared at the glowing candle, focusing on it. A minute passed, the room suddenly growing cold, Odo shivering. "Cold!"

Sephie said, "Too much, focus on the candle, only the candle. Try drawing a circle around the flame with your mind, only absorbing the energy from inside the circle.

Just relax, there's no rush, take your time."

Snow started falling from the ceiling.

"Focus on the candle, nothing else. Draw a bright yellow circle around it."

Twenty seconds later the candle blinked out.

"You did it! Nice job!"

Solis grinned. "Drawing the yellow circle really helped."

"Let's try it again."

An hour later Sephie lit all four candles, Solis blinking them out one at a time. "I don't have to draw the yellow circle anymore."

"That's it, you've got it! Well done. We should go outside for the next part."

The friends headed out into the back yard.

Odo said, "I've never been back here before. These gardens are amazing. How come we have to do it outside?"

"I don't want to burn down Wikerus' house."

"She's lighting a candle, not a bonfire."

Sephie set the candelabra on the ground twenty feet away from Solis, but didn't light the candles.

"Okay, this time I want you to absorb thermal energy from your surroundings, then project it in a very narrow beam, lighting only the candle."

"Can I use the sun?"

"If that's easier for you."

Solis looked up at the sun for a few seconds, holding

her arms out, her body glowing brightly. Odo shielded his eyes from the brilliant light. "Why is she so bright? I think the sun is too–"

A blinding pulse of white hot light blasted out from Solis' hands, the candles and candelabra instantly vaporized, leaving a ten foot wide circle of charred ground, the river stones on the garden path glowing red, the air above them wavering from the heat.

Odo studied the black smoking ground. "On second thought, excellent idea to do it outside."

"That was incredible, but maybe this time don't use the sun. Just absorb enough energy to light the candle."

It took almost two hours of practicing, and three minor fires, but finally Solis could light a single candle from over fifty feet away, sending out a narrow beam of thermal energy from one finger.

"That's perfect, and it's enough for today. We'll come by after school tomorrow and practice some more."

"I'll practice lighting candles tonight. Fox said we would need my powers to survive in my home world. He said I have to be able to control them."

"See you tomorrow. You did great."

Odo and Sephie headed home, strolling down Expergo Street.

Sephie said, "That was a little scary."

"Why? I think her power is cool. She could keep your house warm during the winter and you'd save a ton of money on–"

"You saw what happened when she looked at the sun for two or three seconds. What would happen if she looked at it for ten minutes, or an hour, or a day?"

"She could vaporize a building?"

"Or a city. Maybe a planet."

"How much energy do you think she can absorb?"

"Absorbing the energy didn't seem to bother her, she just glowed like a light bulb. I don't know what her limits are, or if she even has any."

A glimmer of understanding appeared in Odo's eyes. "She's a weapon, a living weapon. She could destroy a planet if she absorbed enough sunlight, enough thermal energy."

"And that's why the Sinarians took her away from her world. They knew how powerful she would become. Can you imagine if anyone on this world learned how to control or replicate her powers?"

"Wikerus said we'd know when it was time to act. I say it's time to take her back to her world."

"I agree, but I should practice with her for a few more days. She's really smart, a fast learner. It won't take her long."

"Do you think everyone on her planet has thermal powers like hers?"

"I don't think so. I don't think a civilization could survive if everyone had powers like that."

"You're right, some crazy dictator would get mad and obliterate the world."

"And if everyone had her powers, the Sinarians wouldn't have taken her from her world."

"Which makes me wonder how and where she got her powers."

"Another mystery. I wish she could remember something about her world."

"Fox said there would be chaos on her world. I can only imagine what he meant by that."

"It doesn't sound good, whatever it is. Her world must be a violent one, maybe post apocalyptic. I wonder how cold she can make things?"

"If it was absolute zero, she could stop all molecular motion."

"Four hundred and fifty-nine degrees below zero. If she could do that, she could either vaporize a planet with a beam of thermal energy, or she could freeze it to absolute zero, wiping out all life in an instant."

"This is getting scary. Four days and then we go. We can't risk her falling into the wrong hands, especially someone like Professor Beauvais. The good news is, now we know the real reason our work rings led us to the flower show and to the sampler."

Chapter 15

See You Later

After four days of training with Sephie, Wikerus and Mrs. Preke decided Solis was ready to return to her home world to face the chaos and obstacles Fox had warned her about.

The five friends took the city bus to Pravus University, making their way to the Reiss Science Center, watching a steady stream of students come and go through the main doors.

Odo gave Sephie a questioning look. "Wouldn't it be easier if we went at night when no one was here? Suppose someone sees us, or follows us through the portal?"

"You told your mom we're going to the movies, right?"

"I did, but why are we here during the day?"

"Because I have a plan."

Solis said, "What kind of plan?"

"It's an excellent, foolproof plan."

Odo groaned. "Which means it's incredibly scary and we're probably all going to die."

"The amount of fear a person experiences in any situation depends on numerous factors. Let's say you're a professional rock climber and you–"

"I didn't say I was scared, I said your plan was scary. What is your plan?"

Silas said, "We're still going through the portal, right?"

"We are, but Odo and I will go in first, both of us translucent so no one will see us. We'll sneak into the lab, take care of the guards and whoever else is in there, then free the alien formshifter and send him home through the portal."

Emmy nodded. "Then we go in?"

"We'll open the lab doors for you as soon we're done. After that it should only take us a few minutes to open the portal to Solis' world."

Odo shrugged. "That's not so scary. Let's do it."

"I told you it was foolproof." Sephie slipped on her Sinarian ring, becoming translucent.

The two friends headed through the main doors, bobbing and weaving past unseeing students. Sephie whispered, "Do you ever get used to dodging people so they don't crash into you?"

"I don't even think about it anymore."

"Here we are."

"Work your magic, Translucent Boy."

"As you wish, Encephalo Girl, although technically it's science, not magic." Odo pressed his hand against the heavily armored lab doors, a shimmering rectangle appearing.

Sephie looked around, then stepped through into the lab, Odo right behind her. She motioned for him to stop, pulling a spray can from her pack.

"What's that for?"

"Black paint for the cameras. So they won't see Silas and Emmy when they come in."

She reached up, spraying black paint on the camera lens. They headed down the hallway, peering into the portal room through the window. Odo whispered, "It's empty. We're in luck."

Sephie pointed down the corridor. "Guard."

"He looks tired, like he needs a nice long nap."

Sephie scanned the guard's brainwaves, sending an electrical impulse to his hypothalamus, stimulating his sleep center. He yawned once, then closed his eyes, sinking slowly to the floor.

"Nighty night."

They crept forward, Odo whispering, "Cameras, over there."

"Got it. Let's go find the prisoner."

They strode down the hallway, Sephie spraying the last two cameras, walking past the sleeping guard and through a heavy metal door. "Those three doors look a lot like prison cells."

Sephie peered through a small round thick glass window into the first room. "Empty."

"So is this one."

Sephie looked into the last room. "Bingo."

"How do we do this?"

"You go in and get him."

"What? Didn't you say he was a scary crocodile guy?"

"Just do it."

"Fine." Odo pressed his hand against the door, stepping through the translucent rectangle, his eyes on the portly man in the rumpled brown tweed suit. "Hey, there, how's it going?"

The man looked up in surprise, squinting, trying to see where the voice was coming from. "What are you?"

"I'm translucent, and we're sending you back to your world."

The man stood up. "Is this a trick?"

"Not a trick. We're rescuing you. Follow me."

They stepped through the shimmering cell door, the man focusing on Sephie. "You're both translucent beings? I don't understand. Who are you? Where are you from?"

Sephie said, "Why are you here? Why did you come to our world?"

"It's what I do, I've visited many worlds. I study lifeforms and cultures on alien worlds. It's quite fascinating. I've written many books about them, they're quite popular in my world."

Odo said, "You're not here to enslave humans and

take all our cool stuff?"

"To be painfully honest, there's nothing here worth taking. Your world is exquisitely primitive, I'm afraid."

Odo nodded. "Got it. Let's get you home. What's your name?"

"I'm Bob, I sell used cars." He grinned, giving Odo a wink.

They hurried back down the hallway past the sleeping guard, following Odo through the door into the portal room.

Sephie darted over to the control panel and grabbed the remote, handing the blue crystal sphere to Bob.

"Hold this."

One by one four buttons on the remote lit up. "All good, we have four symbols." She pressed them in the correct order, the control panel blinking on. "This should do it."

Seconds later the shimmering portal appeared, Odo eyeing the shadowy water world. "That's where you live?"

"Home sweet home." Bob flickered, transforming into a humanoid crocodile.

Odo studied his scaly form, looking for gills. "You're amphibious, able to live on land and in the water?"

"The short answer is yes, I can live on the land or in the water, but it's far more complicated than that."

"It always is. See you later." Odo almost added the word *alligator*, but decided it would be extremely inappropriate. And Sephie would murder him with a big axe.

"Thank you both so much. You saved my life. Others here haven't been so lucky. If I can ever repay you, let me know."

"No problem, we're the Odd Squad, it's what we do."

Sephie gave an internal eye roll.

"My heartfelt thanks to the Odd Squad then." The amphibious alien stepped through the portal, slipping silently into the dark murky water, disappearing from sight.

"Time to open the lab doors."

They ran down the hallway, Odo sliding the door open. When the hallway was empty, Silas, Emmy, and Solis stepped into the lab. After she closed the doors, Sephie drew two symbols in the air, a small silver beam weapon appearing in her hand.

"What's that for?"

"I thought I'd lock the doors before we leave." She aimed the gun at the gray biosensor panel, melting it with a brilliant beam of green light. "The electronics are fried. We're good to go, no one is getting through those doors."

They ran down the hallway into the portal room, Solis eyeing the array of quantum computers. "What is this place? Are those computers, like the one Wikerus has?"

"They're called quantum computers, super powerful. They'll tell us where you're from, and open a portal to your world."

Sephie handed the blue crystal sphere to Solis. "Hold this for a minute."

She pressed the four glowing symbols in the correct order, then the matching symbols on the main control panel, watching as the shimmering portal blinked on, an image appearing. Odo's eyes widened when he saw it. "That's not good."

Silas turned to Sephie. "What do we do? We can't go in there, we won't last five minutes."

Solis cried out, "Something is happening to my medallion!"

Chapter 16

Through the Portal

Odo's eyes were on the frigid raging maelstrom on the other side of the shimmering portal. "We'll freeze to death in two minutes if we go in there. It's a total white out, I can't even tell what kind of world it is."

Silas nodded, "It looks like the blizzards they have in Antarctica."

"We won't freeze if we have the right gear." Sephie drew four symbols, a heavy winter coat appearing. She handed it to Odo. "Try it on."

Odo slipped the coat on. "It fits. You're sure this will be warm enough? It looks seriously cold in there."

"It's made with a high tech fabric that drastically reduces heat loss. You'll be toasty warm, I promise. Elia told me about it when we were on Varania. She helped create the fabric for the Varanian military using artificial reality."

"Nice."

Solis said, "I don't get cold. I never wore a coat, not even on the coldest of winter days."

"You were probably drawing thermal energy from sunlight to keep yourself warm."

Fifteen minutes later the adventurers were fully dressed in Sephie's high tech arctic gear; coats, snow pants, gloves, boots, hats, face masks, and anti-fog snow goggles.

Sephie touched the lab wall, studying it. "Odo, do you notice anything interesting about these walls?"

Odo eyed the smooth metallic surface. "They're made out of aluminum?"

"Bingo. Do you know why?"

Odo shook his head. "Not a clue."

Silas said, "To protect the room from electromagnetic pulse attacks, otherwise known as EMPs."

"Oh, right, aluminum blocks them."

Sephie drew half a dozen symbols, a six-inch round copper colored sphere appearing in her hand.

"What is that?"

"It's the second half of Mrs. Preke's wish list. Part one was sending Bob back to his home world. Part two is making sure no one follows us and no one ever uses this portal again."

"What is that thing? What does it do?"

Sephie pointed to a small red button on the side of the copper sphere. "One minute after I press this button, it will produce an extremely powerful EMP. The aluminum walls will contain it, but every piece of electronic equipment inside this room will be completely fried, totally useless, including all the quantum computers."

"Professor Beauvais said it was the only one in the world and it would take them ten years to rebuild it. That should give us plenty of time."

Silas laughed. "We should get going."

"Solis, what did you say about your medallion?"

"It's glowing, making a buzzing sound."

"It started when the portal opened?"

Solis nodded.

"That's a good thing, it means this is the right world. I think your medallion is meant to guide us."

"Guide us to what?"

"I don't know. Maybe to your home."

Sephie said, "You guys go through first. I'll be right behind you."

"Wait, I want to make sure we're not stepping into an ocean or something." Odo put one foot through, tapping the ground on the other side. "It's solid, we're good."

The four friends stepped through the portal into the ferocious storm, Odo adjusting his goggles. He leaned into the shrieking wind, hollering, "This storm is crazy! I'm not cold though, I don't even feel it."

Sephie waved to them through the portal, then tapped the button on the EMP device and rolled it across the floor. She darted through the rippling gateway, running over to the others.

"All set!"

Exactly one minute later the shimmering blue portal

vanished.

"It worked, their machine is history. They can't follow us."

"Nice. Mrs. Preke will be happy."

"Why is this place so cold? This storm is brutal!"

"It must be an ice planet."

"Or we could be at the north pole."

"Everyone hold hands so we don't get separated in the blizzard. Solis, is your medallion doing anything?"

She held it up to her ear. "It's quiet, but still glowing."

"Turn slowly in a circle, see if anything happens."

She turned, stopping abruptly. "It's buzzing again, vibrating, and the light went from yellow to violet."

"Turn more."

"It's stronger, the light is bright violet. Now it's less."

"We go in whatever direction makes the medallion buzz the loudest and the light glow violet. You lead the way, we'll follow. Everyone hold hands, don't let go."

The friends huddled together for a moment, Odo saying, "How far do you think we have to go?"

Silas said, "I'm guessing maybe ten thousand miles?"

"Very funny."

"We'll follow the medallion until we get there."

"Are we there yet? Are we there yet?"

Emmy turned, laughing, then stopped. "Did you see that? Something in the sky glowed brightly for about two seconds."

"What was it?"

"I have no idea, but it must have been really bright if I could see it through the blowing snow."

"Another unsolved mystery. Let's go."

The adventurers followed Solis through the raging storm, Odo trying to wipe the snow off his goggles with his sleeve. "I'm staying nice and warm. How cold do you think it is here? I wish we had a thermometer."

Silas answered, "It's crazy ridiculous cold."

Emmy called out, "Solis, you're really not cold at all?"

"I don't get hot or cold. I don't know why. My mother always told me it was my angel powers."

Odo stopped, rubbing his foot against the ground. "The ground is smooth here, like a road maybe?"

They trekked on through the buffeting winds and blinding snow for over an hour, the storm abating slightly. "I think it's warming up a bit. It's not snowing as hard and the wind is dying down."

Silas squinted, peering through the falling snow. "Are those buildings?"

"I think it's a city. This is good, it's not just a big desolate ice world. We have to be careful, we don't know what kind of creatures live here."

They crept forward, a vast sprawling metropolis revealing itself as the snowfall continued to diminish. Odo looked up. "I can see the sun. Actually, I can see two of them."

"Cool, a circumbinary world."

"Said the king of nerds."

"Circumbinary means the planet has two suns."

"But no daughters?"

"Hold on, I have to shut off my dad joke alarm."

Emmy was eyeing the glistening ice covered city. "They have skyscrapers, but I don't see anyone, there are no lights and no movement. It looks totally deserted."

"Maybe there was a war."

"The buildings don't look damaged, just frozen."

Solis said, "We keep following this big street."

"Check out those old vehicles next to that blue building."

"They don't have wheels. They must be antigrav cars. That's high tech stuff."

"Maybe they still work. How cool would that be?" Odo darted over to one of the abandoned vehicles, scraping the frost and snow off a side window, peering inside. He gave a horrified screech, jumping back.

"What is it, what did you find?"

"Not good. People, they're frozen solid. Frozen people."

Emmy looked at Sephie. "How could that happen? How could they freeze? Why didn't they go somewhere warm?"

"I don't know, maybe they froze before they–"

Odo gave a yelp. "Over there! Look out!"

Chapter 17

Bandits

"The adventurers spun around, their eyes on a group of rough looking humanoids emerging from a low gray building. One of them stopped when he spotted the Odd Squad, calling out to the others, pointing to the group of adventurers.

"They look like bandits. They have weapons, beam guns."

"I can't see their faces, they're wearing those big furry hoods. They have two arms and two legs though."

Before anyone could stop her, Solis stepped out in front of Odo, eyeing the band of disheveled aliens.

They pointed at her, shrieking out a warning, two of them turning and running. One of the bandits raised a beam weapon, aiming it at Solis. Sephie screamed, "Beam weapon!"

There was a brilliant flash of light, a purple beam sizzling through the frigid air, hitting Solis squarely in the chest. What happened next was something Odo would never forget.

Solis flared brightly with a brilliant violet light. The bandit's weapon flashed a second time, hitting her again. She was barely visible now, obscured by the blindingly bright sphere of raging light surrounding her.

Emmy cried out, "What's happening to her?"

Solis held out both hands, a powerful blast of purple light streaking toward the bandits, hitting the exterior of the building three feet above their heads, vaporizing a six foot wide smoking hole in the wall. The aliens turned and ran, disappearing behind the building.

Solis looked around, her voice a whisper. "What happened? What did I do?"

Sephie said, "You absorbed the energy from the bandit's beam weapon, then projected it back. It blasted that big hole in the building."

"I didn't even think about it, I just did it. I had to protect you."

"You saved our lives."

Silas said, "They were terrified of you. They started screaming when they saw you."

"Did they think I was a forest witch?"

"I don't think that was it."

"They won't bother us again, that's for sure."

"Let's keep going. Everyone keep your eyes open in case there are more of them."

The adventurers forged on, staying close to the buildings.

"We can duck in a doorway and hide if we need to."

Silas stepped over to one of the windows, scraping off the ice and peering inside, his smile vanishing. "I'm not ducking in there. Don't look."

"What is it?"

"Frozen people, a lot of them. Some of them are still standing."

"What?" Odo couldn't help himself, he peered into the store. "That's horrible. It must have happened so fast they never even knew what..." He didn't finish his sentence.

Silas turned to Solis, saying, "They have white hair, just like yours."

"Why would they freeze like that?"

Solis said, "Maybe someone has the same powers I do."

Odo and Sephie glanced at each other, but said nothing.

They trekked on for another hour, finally reaching the outskirts of the city.

Silas looked up at the sky. "It's a miracle, it finally stopped snowing. I think it's actually warming up."

"Solis, what's your medallion doing? Is it still glowing?"

"It is." She turned slowly, listening to the buzzing medallion, watching the light turn violet. "We follow that road."

Half an hour later Silas stopped, taking his arctic gear off, stuffing it into his pack. "I'm getting hot. It's warm out, and there's grass on the ground. Well, purple stuff that looks sort of like grass."

"What are those things?" Emmy pointed to half a dozen eight-inch wide pale green undulating translucent spheres bobbing up and down near a tall spiky tree.

Odo grimaced. "How creepy is that? They're attached to that vine. What are they?"

"Go poke one with your finger and see what happens."

"Very funny."

Sephie cried out, "It's moving!"

Odo let out a yelp when one of the orbs broke free, floating upward, drifting toward him, carried by the breeze. "What's it doing?"

Silas said, "It must be how the vines multiply, how they spread their seeds, the same way dandelion seeds get carried by the wind."

"Except it's super creepy."

"It's just another form of evolutionary adaptation."

Odo jumped back when the thick vine started wriggling across the ground. "It's moving! This is seriously creepy. They had vines just like this in *Return of the Sinister Sorcerer.* They grabbed people and dragged them into a crocodile infested swamp and no one ever saw them again."

Sephie said, "Sorry, Odo, but that was the dumbest movie ever made. None of it made sense, the science was ridiculous."

Odo glared at her. "If by dumb you mean super scary and awesome. Everyone likes the Sinister Sorcerer movies."

Silas nodded. "They are pretty good. Those vines were scary."

Solis pointed to a winding trail leading through the forest. "We follow that path."

"The suns are starting to set. The big one is almost down to the horizon."

Sephie pointed to a clearing ahead of them. "That's a good spot to set up camp for the night. I'll shape sleeping bags and tents."

Odo gave a loud yelp, ducking down when a floating vine orb drifted past his head. "So creepy! I don't like those things."

"It must have lighter than air gas in it, like helium or hydrogen. More than likely it's hydrogen produced by photosynthetic electrolysis." Silas gently tapped one of the orbs as it drifted by. "It's neutrally buoyant, doesn't go up or down. The surface feels a little bit sticky. It's super cool how it floats like that."

Odo said, "Right, super cool. I am totally sleeping in a tent. I don't want one of those things to land on my face while I'm asleep and suck my brains out."

Sephie laughed.

Emmy pointed to a large dark blue vine wrapped around one of the spiky trees. "Look at those pink flowers. They're really pretty."

"We should take some seeds back to Mrs. Beasley. She'd win a big prize at the flower show."

Odo grinned. "A gold medal for the plant that ate the most people."

Solis burst out laughing, quickly covering her mouth, giving an embarrassed look. "I'm sorry, I didn't mean to laugh so loudly. It was an amusing comment."

Sephie smiled. It was the first time she'd seen Solis laugh.

Sephie shaped two large freshly baked veggie pizzas for dinner, the friends eating and chatting until both suns had dipped below the horizon.

"We need a campfire."

Sephie drew four symbols, a ring of stones appearing, then a roaring fire.

"Thanks, Seph."

Solis gazed at the flickering flames. "This reminds me of the stone fireplace in our house. I wish I knew where the medallion was taking us. It's frightening not knowing what will happen next. When I lived in the forest I knew everything about my world. I always knew what to expect, what to watch out for."

Emmy pointed to something behind Solis. "You have a visitor."

Solis turned, a wide smile appearing on her face. "Fox! It is such a comfort to see you, dear friend."

Fox lay down next to her, resting his chin on her leg, closing his eyes as she stroked his soft white fur.

Half an hour later Odo headed for his tent. "So tired, wake me in two days." He closed the tent flaps and crawled into his sleeping bag.

He was sound asleep when the purple vine slithered under the tent door, snaking slowly toward him, its lovely pink blossoms filling the tent with a cloud of pale yellow dust.

Chapter 18

The Cafe

Sephie was sitting across from Odo, gazing up at the clear blue sky. "What a beautiful day. I can't believe we're really here."

"I can't believe we both got full scholarships to Stanford. We are so lucky. I love my classes, they're so much fun, and I have a 4.0 average."

Sephie nodded. "So do I. The classes are a lot easier than I thought they would be, and everyone is so nice and helpful. This is a lovely sidewalk cafe, I'm glad we found it. It's fun to sit out here and watch the people go by. So relaxing. This sandwich is delicious, maybe the best one I've ever had. We should come here again."

Odo nodded. "Absolutely. Mine is super good too. This might be the best day ever."

Sephie reached across the table, taking Odo's hand in hers. "I love you, Odo Whitley."

"I love you, too, Sephie Crumb."

"When I first saw you it felt like I was remembering you, like I've always known you. I knew we were connected somehow. Sometimes I have glimpses, flashes of memories from long ago. I'm with someone, and I know it's you, but it doesn't look like you."

Odo squeezed Sephie's hand. "Best day ever, Seph."

"Nothing could make it better. Nothing."

Odo glanced up when a tall man in a gray pin striped suit stopped in front of their table, smiling at them.

"What a lovely young couple you are. This is for you. Have a fantastic day!" The man set a pink cardboard box down on the table in front of them, giving a cheery wave as he strode off down the sidewalk.

"Who was that guy? He looked a little bit like Wikerus."

"I have no idea. What do you think he gave us?"

"It looks like a box from a bakery. Maybe it's a cake, or pastries."

Odo flipped the lid open, gaping at the stacks of hundred dollar bills and dozens of gleaming gold coins. "Whoa, this is crazy. Look at all those gold coins."

Sephie studied the contents of the box, a frown crossing her face. "Something's not right."

"What do you mean? What's not right? This is amazing, that guy gave us a zillion dollars."

"Everything is too perfect, it's too amazing, too fantastic. It's too much."

Odo furrowed his brow. "Now that you mention it, I don't remember applying to Stanford. That's kind of weird."

He turned to look at Sephie, but she was gone. He spun around again. The sky was dark, ominous, the streets empty. His anxiety spiked, a feeling of dread rolling through him. "Sephie? Where are you? Sephie!"

He wriggled when he felt something invisible wrapping around him, the cafe vanishing. Maybe he was having a dream, maybe he was all wrapped up in his blanket. It was getting tighter, hard to breathe. "What is this, what's happening? I have to wake up!" He forced himself to open his eyes.

"Gahh, what is this stuff?" He clawed at the soft silky white blanket pressed against his face. "Eww, it's like a cocoon or something. So creepy. What is happening?" He wriggled wildly, trying to break free of the horrifying white shroud, then stopped. He could feel himself swinging back and forth, like a pendulum. "I'm hanging from something! Wait, I know what to do!" He twisted his arm, pressing his hand against the cocoon wall, making a translucent doorway.

"No good, I still can't move, and I'm way up in a tree." He squirmed wildly, trying to break free of the cocoon. "It's too strong. What is this stuff?" He took a deep breath, then yelled as loud as he could, "HELP! HELP!"

He yelled until his voice was hoarse, his cries muffled by the thick white blanket wrapped around him. He listened for a reply, but none came. "This is bad. Maybe that creepy vine did this, maybe it dragged me out of my tent, maybe it's carnivorous, maybe it eats people. It's just like the Sinister Sorcerer movie!"

Odo tried to contain his panic. "I have to relax, I have to think. The vine probably drugged me, made me sleep and have super happy dreams, then wrapped me in this silk cocoon. Sephie told me in the dream that we were connected somehow, maybe across time. I felt that too, even before the dream." Only a few weeks ago Silas had told him that some scientists think the human brain functions like an organic quantum computer, and that telepathy occurs when two minds are entangled on the quantum level. If his deeper self was entangled with Sephie's, maybe he could send his thoughts to her, maybe she'd hear them. He concentrated deeply, sending out his message.

"Sephie! This is Odo, I need your help! I'm wrapped up in a cocoon, hanging from a tree. Help me! The vine's going to eat me!"

For the next ten minutes he sent the same message over and over.

Sephie's eyes blinked open. Something was very wrong, she felt sick inside, frightened. It was Odo, something was wrong with Odo! She jumped out of her sleeping bag, pulled her clothes on, and ran out of the tent, crying out, "ODO!" She raced over to his tent, eyeing the torn flaps, peering inside. He was gone.

Silas crawled out of his tent, rubbing his eyes. "What is it? What are you yelling about?"

"Odo's gone! I was having a dream about him, then

something bad happened. He's in danger, I know he is. We have to find him!"

"Where did he go?"

Solis and Emmy stepped out of their tent, running over to Sephie and Silas. "What happened to Odo?"

"We don't know, but his tent is torn and he's gone. Maybe one of those vines grabbed him."

Sephie shaped a flashlight, moving the beam across the ground in front of Odo's tent.

"There, drag marks. Something dragged him from the tent in that direction."

"Hurry, we have to find him!"

The four friends followed the drag marks to the base of a huge spiky tree, a massive purple vine wound around it. Sephie moved the flashlight beam slowly up the fifty-foot tall trunk. She gave a start when she saw the white cocoon hanging from a branch high above them. She screamed, "ODO! ODO!"

There was a muffled reply, barely audible. "I'm up here! Help! I think it's going to eat me!"

"We see you! Hold on!"

"We're going to get you down!"

Silas studied the cocoon. "We can't climb the tree because of the vine."

Emmy said, "I'll fly up and bring him down."

"Be careful, watch out for the vine, don't let it grab you."

Emmy converted her physical body into a dream

body, the same body she created in her dreams at night.

"Be right back." She drifted up, staying clear of the huge wriggling vine. Seconds later she pressed her hands against the cocoon, calling out, "Odo, it's Emmy! I'm going to fly you back down."

She made the cocoon become part of her dream body, but she couldn't pull it away from the tree. She gave a cry when she saw the huge vine wriggling up the trunk toward her.

Silas cried out, "Watch out for the vine!" He spotted a cloud of orange dust spewing out of the pink blossoms. "Look out! Don't breathe the orange dust! It might be poisonous!"

Solis held out both hands, her body glowing brightly. The vine stopped moving, suddenly covered with ice, snow drifting down from above.

Sephie called out, "Odo, Solis froze the vine!"

Emmy hollered down to them, "I can't move the cocoon, it's hanging from a big thick rope thing. I can't break it."

"Hold on to the cocoon, I'll burn the rope." Solis pointed a finger at the top of the cocoon, a narrow beam of brilliant white light shooting out, vaporizing the white silken rope, separating the cocoon from the tree.

Two minutes later Sephie and Silas were pulling Odo out of the cocoon. Sephie grabbed his hand. "Are you okay?"

"You heard me? You heard my thoughts?"

Sephie nodded. "Something woke me up, I knew something was wrong. We followed the drag marks to the tree and saw you up there."

Odo got to his feet, staring at the tree. "I knew those crazy vines were dangerous, they're exactly like the ones in the Sinister Sorcerer that drag people into the crocodile swamp."

"Except the vines in the movie didn't put people into cocoons."

"And there are no crocodiles here. But other than that, it's exactly the same."

Emmy whispered, "And no swamp either. Sorry, Odo."

Chapter 19

The Gorge

Odo slept in the next morning, exhausted from his terrifying cocoon experience, awakening to the sound of talking and laughter. He peered out of his tent, spotting the others sitting around a campfire. Throwing his clothes on, he stepped over to the fire, taking a seat next to Sephie.

"What's for breakfast? I'm starving."

"You mean what's for lunch?"

"It's lunchtime? That orange dust really makes you sleep. Hey, we should take some of those flowers back with us. I bet the pharmaceutical companies would pay a fortune for something that makes you have amazing dreams like–"

Sephie whacked his arm. "Worst idea ever."

Silas nodded. "That's the last thing people need."

"Good point. Everyone would dream their life away, never do anything."

"We should pack up our gear and head out. Only ten thousand more miles to go."

"Ha ha. I wonder how far it really is? And where we're going?"

"Wherever it is, it has something to do with Solis."

After a quick lunch, they packed up their gear and headed down the forest trail.

Half an hour later Silas heard Sephie call out, "Swordfish!"

Odo yelled, "Correct!"

"Oak tree!"

"Correct!"

"Dinosaur!"

Silas stopped. "What are you two doing?"

"We're sending thoughts to each other. I think of a word and I send it to her. Pretty soon we won't need phones, we'll just send thought messages to each other."

"Right." Silas glanced at Sephie, then back to Odo.

Odo frowned. "What? Why are you looking like that?"

Silas stepped closer to Odo, whispering, "You're really sure you want to do that?"

"Do what?"

"You really want to know what each other is thinking?"

"Sure, why not?"

"Suppose you get her a present and she thinks it's dumb? She couldn't pretend she liked it, and you'd have to go buy something else because you'd feel bad about her not liking it. And what happens if she's watching you dance and she thinks you look like someone who stumbled into a spider web in a haunted house?"

"What's that supposed to mean? I'm an excellent dancer."

Sephie called out, "It does look a little like that, Odo."

Odo made a face at Sephie, then laughed. "Maybe Silas is right. We should only send our thoughts in dire emergencies."

"I agree, dire emergencies only. Like if we wanted to have an emergency lunch at a little sidewalk cafe."

Odo froze. Had Sephie been sharing the cafe dream with him? Had she been there? Did she remember all the mushy stuff they said? "Sidewalk cafe? Why would you say that?"

"No reason, I just meant if we wanted to go have lunch somewhere."

"You could text me, that might be easier."

Silas called out, "I think we're almost through the forest."

They strolled along the trail, Odo scanning the thinning foliage. "Not so many trees here, and those crazy vines are gone. Those things were totally scary."

The friends stopped when they saw the massive milewide gorge in front of them.

Odo dropped his pack on the rocky ground with a thump, staring at the monumentally wide gorge. "What is it with giant gorges? Every time we visit a world, there's a stupid giant gorge blocking our path, like that one in Pangaea. Whoever invented giant gorges should be boiled in–"

Silas stepped over to the edge, peering down into the gorge. "It's not just a gorge, I think it's a divide between two tectonic plates. I can't see the bottom, but I can feel heat coming up from the magma. It's like what we saw in Pangaea."

"No problem, it's only a mile across, I'll just jump over to the other side."

Solis stared at Odo. "You can jump that far?"

Sephie laughed. "In his dreams maybe."

"Emmy can fly us across."

Emmy nodded, grabbing Silas' hand. "Let's do it, everyone hold hands and I'll fly us over."

A minute later everyone had a shimmering translucent dream body. Everyone except Solis.

"Why isn't Solis translucent?"

"I don't know. Let me try it with just her." Emmy took Solis' hand. She transformed to her dream body, but Solis was still solid. "I don't know why it's not working."

"There must be something about her body that's preventing it. Maybe the way she absorbs energy?"

"So what do we do now?"

"We'll have to find another way across, look for a bridge, or we could go around the gorge."

Emmy floated up into the air. "It looks narrower down that way. I'll fly along the gorge and look for a place to cross over."

"Be careful, we don't know what's out there."

"I will." She flew off, disappearing into the distance.

The friends took a seat on the rocky ground.

"Which way is your medallion pointing?"

"It's pointing across the gorge. I wish I could remember something about this world. I don't like feeling lost."

"We always get lost on our adventures. You get used to it, we'll be fine. Besides, we're not really lost because we have your medallion to guide us. I totally trust the Sinarians."

Emmy hadn't returned after almost an hour, and Silas was beginning to worry. "Why is she taking so long? Do you think something happened to her? Should we go check on her?"

Solis pointed to a small speck in the sky. "There she is! She's okay!"

"You can see her from here?"

"My mom used to say I had angel eyes."

A minute later Emmy landed, waving to them. "We're good! I found a bridge, a big one."

"Nice. How far is it?"

"Fifteen or twenty miles. There's something else though." She gave a nervous laugh, her eyes darting over to Silas.

Odo frowned. "What kind of something else? Are there more of those vines? Crazy monsters?"

"It's two things, really. The bridge crosses the gorge, but it also goes into a big tunnel on the other side. We have to go through the tunnel, and I have no idea what's in there."

"What's the second thing?"

"Um, we have to go through an orchard?"

"What's scary about an orchard? We can get some fresh fruit."

"Well…"

Odo's eyes narrowed. "What? What kind of orchard is it?"

"The kind where the trees can walk?"

"What?"

"The trees are walking around and it looks like they're packing fruit into wooden boxes."

"You're saying walking trees are harvesting their own fruit and packing it into boxes?"

"That's what it looks like."

"That's totally weird, but not exactly scary. They could be genetically engineered hybrid plants. Not that weird."

Silas stood up, slinging his pack onto his shoulder. "This sounds fun, I've always wanted to see a walking tree."

"I've never heard anyone say that before."

They headed along the edge of the gorge, Odo and Sephie holding hands.

Emmy stopped short. "Oh, I almost forgot, there were big robots there too, but I don't know what they were doing."

Odo spun around. "You almost forgot big robots? What kind of big robots?"

"I don't know, just really big silver ones."

Chapter 20

The Brimble Thief

Odo was still questioning Emmy about the orchard as they trekked along the massive chasm. "You're certain you saw trees walking? It wasn't an old amusement park with animated trees, or weird robots that looked kind of like trees?"

"The trees were walking, and there were lots of them. They had branches and roots and leaves and fruit. And there were some big silver robots walking around the orchard. I think they were in charge of the trees, telling them what to do."

"Right." Odo peered over into the gorge, frowning. "I can't even see the bottom of the gorge."

"Technically, it's not a gorge, it's a divergent boundary. It's caused by tectonic plates moving apart, like when Pangaea split apart and formed the continents we have today. I did a lot of research on Pangaea after we went there."

"Thanks, Professor Silas, that was most informative."

"Big test tomorrow. Make sure you study."

Five heads turned when they heard the scuffling, rattling sounds coming from behind them. They spun around, jumping to one side, gaping at the twenty foot tall tree running toward them, its branches flailing wildly, a large wooden wagon bouncing along behind it.

When it had passed, Emmy grinned. "Gosh, what was that thing? Wait, was that a walking tree? It kind of looked like one, didn't it? A walking tree?"

Odo's jaw was hanging open.

Silas said, "Technically it was a running tree, not a walking tree."

"It was running on its roots, using them like legs. That's crazy."

"What was in that wagon it was pulling?"

"A bunch of wooden crates."

"One of them was open, I think it was full of nails."

Sephie kneeled down, picking something up. "Bingo, a big silver nail. "

Emmy said, "The trees were loading fruit into wooden boxes just like the ones in the wagon. There were hundreds of boxes, maybe thousands."

"They might use the nails to build the wooden crates."

Odo said, "The tree didn't seem that scary, just in a big hurry to get somewhere. I'm not too worried."

The friends continued on, Odo speculating on the nature of the walking trees. "They're probably not real trees, more like bioform androids that have been engineered to grow fruit."

Solis said, "It looked like a real tree. It had leaves and branches and roots and bark."

Odo gave Sephie a sideways glance. "Speaking of trees, does anyone know which tree has the most bark?"

Sephie groaned. "No tree jokes, please."

Silas said, "Seriously, no tree jokes. I'm begging you."

"Fine, but it's the dogwood tree. Get it? The most *bark*? *Dogwood*?"

"One more joke like that and we're throwing you into the divergent boundary."

Solis stopped, whispering, "Look!"

The friends ducked down behind a boulder, peering out at the vast orchard a few hundred feet ahead of them.

Silas whispered, "It's huge, there are hundreds of trees, maybe thousands."

"And they're all walking."

"Just like I said they were."

"Fine, you were right, they're walking trees."

Odo stepped out from behind the rock. "Let's go check it out. Maybe we can get some free fruit. I like fruit."

Sephie said, "We should be careful. The trees might be harmless, but we don't know about the robots. They could be dangerous."

"It's an orchard, not a super secret military facility."

"We should still be careful."

They walked toward the bustling orchard, watching

the trees pack fruit into long wooden crates.

"They look like apples, except they're oranges."

"Or do they look like oranges, except they're apples?"

"I see what you did there, very clever indeed."

One of the trees began to shake violently, several hundred of the orange apples raining down from its branches, bouncing across the purple grass. A twelve foot tall silver robot stepped out of a wooden shed, its eyes on the trees. "Pack them! Pack them! Keep it moving!"

The trees scurried over to the fallen fruit, quickly gathering it up, placing it into a big wooden crate. A second silver robot darted over, slamming a lid on the crate, nailing it shut with a heavy steel hammer.

Odo whispered, "Now we know what the nails were for."

The silver robot bellowed out, "Stack them! Stack them! Keep it moving!"

The trees grabbed the heavy wooden boxes, carrying them across the orchard to an enormous wall of stacked crates.

"Whoa, look how many crates there are over there."

"There must be ten thousand of them, and that's just the ones we can see."

One of the silver robots stepped over to the adventurers, eyeing them closely. "You are here to transport the brimbles? Where is your ship?"

Odo attempted a friendly smile. "No, we're just...

um… tourists."

"You are not here to pick up the brimbles?"

"We're not. When is the last time someone was here?"

"Nine years ago. Do you have a ship? You're picking up the brimbles?"

"No, we're not picking up the brimbles, we're just out for a pleasant stroll along the gorge."

The robot turned abruptly, walking away.

"Eww, what's that smell?"

"I think it's rotten fruit."

"It's so bad. He said no one has been here to get the fruit for nine years. That's a lot of rotten fruit in those crates."

"Why do they keep working?"

"Because they're mutant alien walking trees with crazy silver robot bosses?"

"I wonder why they stopped coming for the fruit?"

"You saw the city."

"Right, everyone was frozen."

Odo reached down and grabbed one of the orange apples, sniffing it. "He called it a brimble. It smells kind of good, I'm going to try it."

Time seemed to stop when Odo bit into the brimble, a sudden eerie silence descending across the orchard, every tree turning slowly toward Odo. Six huge silver robots were staring at him, their eyes pulsing with a frightening red glow.

"Odo, put the brimble down. The robots don't look

happy."

"It's no big deal, I just took a bite of one that was lying on the–"

One of the robots shrieked, "BRIMBLE THIEF! DESTROY THE BRIMBLE THIEF! KILL HIM! KILL THEM ALL!"

A beam of blazing orange light sizzled across the orchard, missing Odo by inches, the grass behind him bursting into flames. He gave a screech, jumping back, hollering, "It was lying on the ground and I thought it was–"

Sephie flicked her wrist, a shimmering wall of energy surrounding them. A second beam of orange light bounced off her energy shield.

"Run for it!"

The adventurers raced along the edge of the gorge, two of the monstrous silver robots thundering after them, firing their deadly beam weapons at the fleeing companions.

"Faster! They're catching up to us!"

Solis stopped abruptly, turning to face the silver automatons. Both robots fired their weapons, hitting her with blasts of orange light. Her body flared brightly, absorbing the power of the beams. The robots stopped, confused by what they were seeing.

Solis held her arms out, the robots instantly covered with a thick layer of ice, unable to move. Solis' body was glowing like a small sun when a wall of yellow light blasted out from her hands, slamming into the two robots, hurling them backwards head over heels for almost a quarter of a mile.

They lay still for a moment, then staggered to their feet. One of them shook its fist at Solis, then they both turned and ran.

Sephie said, "Odo, would you mind running back and grabbing a basket of brimbles? We could make a brimble pie for dinner. Doesn't that sound good?"

"Those robots are totally insane. Totally. Insane."

"Said the brimble thief."

Chapter 21

The Tunnel

Leaving the brimble orchard and its overzealous guardians behind them, the adventurers pressed on, making their way along the gorge.

"How much farther to the bridge?"

Emmy said, "We're close, not too much more."

Sephie was the first to spot it. "There it is! I see the bridge!"

"It's huge, way bigger than I thought it would be. What do you think they used it for? Do you think it—"

Emmy interrupted Odo. "Why is it so dark?"

Odo glanced behind them, his eyes widening at the sight of a massive wall of rolling black clouds heading toward them. "Giant storm! Look at those crazy black clouds!"

A powerful gust of whipping wind hit them, almost knocking Odo over. "It's going to be bad! We need to get across the bridge and into the tunnel!"

The friends took off running, Silas hollering when a sudden deluge of pounding rain hit them, drenching the friends as they raced toward the bridge.

Odo yelled through the howling wind, "Does anyone have an umbrella I can borrow? A blue one would be nice, but green would be better, or one with yellow stripes."

"You're a lunatic!" Sephie shaped a powerful dome of energy above them, temporarily protecting them from the pounding rain.

"Thanks, Seph!"

They ran along the edge of the gorge, slipping and sliding on the wet rocks, fighting against the roaring wind. Odo stumbled, flailing wildly, Silas grabbing him before he could fall.

"Thanks! I thought I was going into the gorge!"

Emmy called out, "Everyone hold hands so the wind won't blow us over!"

They pushed onward through the screaming gale force winds and pounding rain for almost twenty minutes, finally reaching the huge mile-wide suspension bridge. Odo scrambled onto the massive structure, pointing to three sets of silver rails running toward the tunnel. "They look like train tracks!"

The storm ended as abruptly as it had started, but the air was turning bitterly cold, ice crystals sparkling in the sunlight. "What's happening? Why is it so cold? Solis, are you doing that?"

"It's not me."

Emmy shrieked when golf ball sized hailstones

started falling from the sky, bouncing and clattering off the metal decking of the bridge. Silas gave a yelp of pain when an especially large hailstone collided with his shoulder. Sephie shaped another wall of energy above them, the hailstones careening off, thousands of the icy spheres smashing into jagged shards when they hit the frozen metal deck.

Odo was shivering violently. "I'm freezing! It's so cold!"

Solis glowed brightly, a sphere of warmth radiating around the group of adventurers. "Does that help?"

"Much better, thanks!"

"Hurry, we have to get to the tunnel!"

They pushed on, slipping and sliding across the ice covered surface, finally reaching the shadowy hundred-foot wide tunnel entrance, stumbling inside. Silas leaned over, trying to catch his breath. "That was brutal. Did you see how big those hailstones were? My shoulder still hurts from getting hit."

Emmy called out, "The hail stopped!"

There was a sudden eerie silence, the bridge covered with almost a foot of shattered ice, the rest of the bridge hidden in an impenetrable fog of drifting ice particles.

"There's no way it should get that cold, that fast."

Emmy said, "We would have frozen to death without Solis."

Odo shouted when he saw the pillar of brilliant light shoot up into the sky. "There's that crazy light again, just like the one Emmy saw when we got here!"

Sephie was eyeing the pillar of blazing white hot light. "I know what's happening. Solis was right, there's someone out there with the same powers she has. They're absorbing all the thermal energy from their surroundings, freezing everything, then sending the thermal energy up into space."

"Why are they doing it? Why would they freeze everything? Why kill all those people in the city?"

"Maybe they're alien invaders."

Sephie shook her head. "It doesn't seem like an organized invasion, it feels almost random."

"Whatever it is, it's freaky. Let's get out of here, find out where this tunnel goes."

"Maybe we'll find a train we can take all the way through."

"I keep thinking about those walking trees. Do you think they were intelligent bioforms created by scientists? They clearly understood what the silver robots were telling them to do."

"They could have evolved that way, gaining mobility and intelligence. They have some weird plants here, like the giant vine that tried to eat me."

The friends strolled along the silver tracks, Sephie shaping a glowing orb of light to illuminate the way.

Odo ran his hand along the tunnel wall. "The walls are super smooth, like glass, but it's carved out of solid rock. You'd need some high tech machines to do that, they couldn't do it like this with hammers and chisels. "

"They could have used a vaporizing beam."

"True. They have big skyscrapers and antigrav vehicles, so they must have pretty advanced technology."

"I thought it would be cold in here, but it's getting warmer."

Silas stopped short. "Do you hear that?"

Odo nodded. "It sounds like a machine, a thumping sound."

"Maybe it's a ventilation system. The air in here seems fresh and I can feel a breeze."

The friends came to an abrupt halt when a white-haired man carrying a toolbox stepped out of a dark alcove, turning in surprise when he saw them. He took a step back. "Who are you? What do you want?"

Solis smiled when she saw his white hair and green eyes, stepping forward and waving to him. "Hello!"

The toolbox fell from his hands with a crash, the man backing away. "No, please. Please go away, there are children here, families. Please don't hurt us. Leave us alone!" He turned and ran, disappearing around a wide curve in the tunnel.

Solis stared down the tunnel. "Why was he afraid of me? We're the same, we have white hair and green eyes. I don't understand, I thought he would like me."

"The bandits were terrified of you too. I think there's someone out there who looks like you, and people are terrified of them."

"Someone who looks like me is freezing the cities, killing people?"

Odo nodded. "It would explain why people are so scared of you. They think you're someone else."

Sephie said, "Odo and I will go talk to whoever lives here, tell them they don't need to be afraid of you, that we just want to get through the tunnel."

"We'll stay here with Solis."

"We won't be long."

Odo and Sephie rounded the curve in the tunnel, spotting a cluster of brightly lit wooden buildings ahead of them. The thumping sound was growing louder.

"It's a little town, with lights."

"They're probably hiding in here from whoever is freezing the cities."

"What should we say to them?"

Sephie thought for a moment, then said, "We should ask them for help. That will work."

"Why?"

"So they won't be afraid of us. People like to help people, and scary people don't usually ask for help."

Odo nodded. "Good plan."

Sephie called out, "Can someone help us? Please!"

A few heads poked out of the wooden structures.

A voice echoed down the tunnel. "What do you want? Where is the Ice Child?"

"Who?"

"The Ice Child. We know she's with you, we saw her."

Sephie said, "She's not an Ice Child, and she won't hurt you. She's our friend. We're trying to get through the tunnel, but we're lost."

A white haired woman emerged from one of the buildings, cautiously walking toward them. "I am Mayor Eloi. The Ice Child will not harm us?"

"She's not an Ice Child, she just looks like one. She would never hurt anyone, she's our friend. I promise you."

"You can't get through the tunnel, it's blocked about half a mile from here. Three days ago the old support beams failed, the walls and roof collapsing. Twelve of our people are trapped on the other side. We don't know if they survived, or how badly they're injured."

Odo said, "We can help you."

"How?"

"It's complicated, but we can help."

"Very well, I will grant passage through the tunnel for you and your friends."

Chapter 22

Rescued

Sephie and Odo ran back down the tunnel to get the others.

"The mayor gave us permission to go through the tunnel, but she said it's blocked, the support beams failed and a section of it collapsed. I told her we could fix it, open a path. Solis, don't use your powers here, we told them you're not an Ice Child."

They headed back to the makeshift town, Sephie introducing the others to Mayor Eloi, who seemed unable to take her eyes off Solis as they strolled along the brightly lit tunnel.

"You're really not an Ice Child?"

Solis gave a friendly smile, shaking her head. "No, I am not."

Sephie said, "Why do you think she's an Ice Child?"

The Mayor studied Sephie's face. "Where are you from? I have not seen hair or eyes like yours before."

"We're from another world, a place called Earth."

The mayor nodded, showing no sign of surprise. "I

see. And your friend Solis, where is she from?"

"It's a long story, but we think the Sinarians took her from this world when she was two years old and brought her to our world, but to a different time, over two centuries before us."

"Who are the Sinarians?"

"They're a highly advanced race of beings with incredible powers."

"I see. How long have you been here on Suvon?"

"Not long. We're trying to find Solis' home, find her parents. We had to cross the gorge and this bridge was the only place we could find to do it. "

Odo said, "Your world is called Suvon?"

"It is, and until ten years ago it was an advanced civilization with interstellar travel and remarkable bioengineering technologies."

"What happened ten years ago?"

"The Children of Ice happened. No one knows why they are here. They seem to wander without purpose, without destination, freezing the land around them, no matter if it is a city or a vast empty plain. Their blazing towers of light are a terror to behold, lighting up the sky for a hundred miles. They show no mercy, no fear. Countless thousands of Suvonians have lost their lives to them."

"That's dreadful. You said they look like Solis? That's why you were afraid of her?"

"Few people have seen them and survived, but we

have heard stories. They are identical in size and form to your friend Solis, strangely beautiful, their hair cut short like hers."

"How many Children of Ice are there?"

"We don't know. Our lines of communication were severed years ago, so we know little of what is happening outside our town. We stay hidden here, hoping a Child of Ice will not wander in."

"How is it warm in here?"

"We have a duplonium generator which provides all the electrical energy we need for fresh air and heat."

"You have duplonium on Suvon?"

"It is not found naturally on our world. I believe we import it from a world called Plindor."

Odo glanced at Sephie. They had been to Plindor, sailed with the desert pirates who mine duplonium. That was where they met their friend Cyra, the Fortisian who taught Sephie how to use her powers.

Mayor Eloi said, "The tunnel collapse is just around this bend."

They rounded the curve in the tunnel, Odo studying the massive wall of rock and debris blocking their path. He turned to Sephie. "What do you think?"

Solis said, "Maybe I could–"

Sephie interrupted her, afraid she was going to mention her powers. "I know what to do. I can shape a heavy particle beam weapon that will create a hole in the rubble, one big enough for people to walk through. Once that's done, I'll fuse the surrounding rock so it won't collapse."

Silas set his pack down. "What about the people on the other side? We should warn them about the disruptor beam."

Odo studied the massive pile of jagged rock. "There's too much rock for me to make a translucent doorway."

Silas turned to Sephie. "What about your Traveling Eye?"

"That should work." She took a seat on the ground, leaning back against the tunnel wall, closing her eyes.

Mayor Eloi whispered, "What is she doing?"

"She's using a power called the Traveling Eye to send her consciousness through the rock to the other side. She'll be able to communicate with your friends, warn them about the disruptor beam."

"I have never heard of such a thing."

"Not many people have. Sephie is amazing."

Sephie drifted out of her body and through the massive wall of rubble, spotting a group of people sitting around a small fire.

One of them gave a yelp when she transformed into her blue shimmering spectral body.

"What is that?"

"Is it a ghost?"

"A Child of Ice?"

"I'm not a ghost or a Child of Ice. I'm here to help you. You need to move farther down the tunnel. We're going to vaporize a hole in the rock so you can get back through the tunnel."

"What are you?"

"I'm from another world. This is not my physical body, it is a spectral form which lets me pass through solid objects."

The villagers got up, moving down the tunnel, one of them calling out, "Whoever you are, thank you for helping us."

Sephie passed back through the wall of debris to her body, her eyes blinking open. "All clear, they moved on down the tunnel."

She stood up, motioning for the others to step back.

"Here we go." She drew six intricate symbols, a three foot long deadly particle disruptor beam and a pair of black goggles appearing in front of her. She slipped the goggles on, then grabbed the weapon. "Everyone turn away, close your eyes." She tapped a button, the device making a low humming sound.

A blindingly brilliant purple cone of light blasted out of the weapon, a wide circular section of rocks vaporizing.

"It's working, but it will take me a while to get all the way through."

She slowly moved forward, step by step, advancing through the wall of jagged rock and heavy timbers. Fifteen minutes later she reached the other side, leaving an eight foot wide circular tunnel behind her.

Tapping a second button, she moved the beam slowly across the remaining sections of collapsed wall, fusing the huge boulders together.

She drew two symbols and the beam weapon vanished. "All done! You're good to go!"

The trapped Suvonians ran forward, cheering, Sephie following them back through the tunnel.

Mayor Eloi clapped Sephie on the back, a wide grin on her face. "You have our deepest gratitude. If there is anything we can do to repay you, all you have to do is ask."

Silas said, "Where does the tunnel go? What's on the other side?"

Mayor Eloi's smiled faded. "My answer may not be the one you wish to hear. The tunnel leads to a long abandoned underground military depot. When we first arrived, a few of our people were able to open the armored doors and venture in, but only one returned, the others killed by the Guardians who had survived the great freezing."

"An Ice Child froze the base?"

"It must have wandered in somehow. There were hundreds of fatalities, so many frozen bodies. That was over ten years ago, but Guardians still roam the facility. We hear them moving about from time to time."

"Who are the Guardians? Are they Suvonian soldiers?"

"They are immensely powerful warrior androids,

virtually indestructible, on high alert and programmed to destroy all intruders."

Odo groaned. "Of course they are."

Chapter 23

The Ghost

The five adventurers said their goodbyes to Mayor Eloi and the villagers, heading off down the long tunnel.

"They must have used the tunnel to bring in heavy equipment and supplies to the underground depot. Maybe we'll find an antigrav ship we can use."

"What are we going to do about the Guardians? They sound totally scary."

"Silas, could you take care of that while we have a nice leisurely lunch?"

"I have an idea, why don't you distract them with a hilarious joke while we sneak through the facility."

"Something like, what did the geologist keep in his kitchen cabinet?"

Emmy grinned. "What did he keep in his kitchen cabinet?"

"Don't encourage him, he'll just tell more."

Odo turned to Emmy. "What did he keep in his kitchen cabinet? That's where he kept his tectonic plates. Get it? Tectonic *plates*? In his kitchen cabinet?" Odo slapped his leg, giving a ridiculously loud laugh.

Sephie did a face palm. "Worst ever."

Solis looked puzzled. "What are tectonic plates?"

Silas proceeded to give a detailed explanation of how tectonic plates are created, and how they form the continents found on many worlds. When he was finished, Solis nodded.

"That's very interesting, and now I understand why Odo's joke is funny. The geologist's kitchen cabinet was filled with ordinary dinner plates made of porcelain, but to be humorous, he called them tectonic plates, because he was a geologist and was well versed in such matters."

Odo was searching for a reply when Emmy called out, "We're here! There's the entrance to the underground base!"

They ran ahead, the friends approaching the mammoth vault doors. "Those are huge, at least fifty feet tall."

"And they're open wide enough for us to get in."

Emmy said, "I can fly in and look around, scout the place out, look for Guardians."

Silas' eyes were focused on a shimmering blue ghost leaning against the vault door, a sour look on his face. The ghost gave a start when he saw Silas looking at him.

"You can see me?"

Silas nodded. *"I can. I'm the only one though. How long have you been here?"*

"Since the big freeze. Everyone else moved on, but I stayed behind. I play tricks on the Guardians, watch

them run around like fools when I knock things over. You'll never get past them. You're doomed, all of you. You don't have a prayer. At least I'll have some company. It's not so bad being a ghost. Do you play cards?"

"You can knock things over?"

"I create electromagnetic fields to pull metal objects off the shelves. I was an electrical engineer. It drives the Guardians crazy. It's hilarious. Makes me laugh to see them running around chasing a ghost."

Odo was watching Silas. "Are you talking to a ghost?"

"I am. He's been here since the Child of Ice froze the base."

"Why is he still here?"

"I'm not sure, but he says he plays tricks on the Guardians, makes them run around and try to find him."

"Does he know how to get through the facility? Can he help us?"

Silas turned to the ghost. *"Could you help us get through the depot? We're trying to get up to the surface."*

The ghost studied the group, then said, *"Sure, I can help you. No problem. You'll never make it though, you won't last more than a few minutes. The elevator is on the other side of this level. That will take you topside, if you can reach it. Bright yellow doors, big violet button next to it. Hit the button and you're in. You can't miss it. Unless a Guardian gets you first."*

"What can we do about the Guardians? Is there any

way to get past them?"

"I can distract them while you run for it. It should take you about three minutes if you run fast. Just keep heading in that direction, past all the heavy weapons and vehicles."

"Can we use any of the weapons to stop the Guardians?"

"You could, but you'd obliterate the facility and everyone in it."

"You'll distract them while we run for the elevators?"

"That's what I said, didn't I?"

"Right, sorry, thanks." Silas was getting a bad feeling about the ghost. Something was off about him. Way off.

"No problem. I'll go in and distract them while you and your friends make a run for the elevator." The ghost floated into the facility, an unreadable smile on his face. *"This is going to be fun."*

Silas whispered to the others, "The ghost says he'll distract the Guardians while we run for the elevator, but it doesn't feel right. I think he's up to something. I don't trust him, and he kept saying we're doomed."

"Why is he saying that?"

"He said he'd have some company if the Guardians destroy us, that we could all play cards. That it's not bad being a ghost."

Odo frowned. "That doesn't sound good. He sounds kind of loopy."

"I think he's really angry."

"Did he say what kind of weapons the Guardians have?"

"No, he just said they would obliterate us."

"We know they survived the Ice Child, so Solis probably can't help us."

Emmy said, "I could fly everyone to the elevator, but I can't take Solis."

Odo furrowed his brow, thinking. "Sephie, remember when we sneaked into the royal palace on Varania, and Elia had those PIFs, the personal invisibility fields? Could you shape those for us?"

Sephie nodded. "I can, but they only last for five minutes."

"They can be our backup, in case the ghost can't distract the Guardians."

Sephie drew a series of symbols in the air, then waited. "It's a complex device."

Thirty seconds later, five blinking wrist bands appeared in front of her. She grabbed one, putting it on her wrist. "Violet button activates it, yellow shuts it off. It works for five minutes, then takes ten minutes to recharge."

"The ghost said we can make it to the elevator in three minutes if we run."

Sephie tapped the violet button and vanished, reappearing a few seconds later. "Did it work?"

"It worked, you were invisible."

"Everyone put one on."

Odo jumped when he heard a stupendous crash from inside the facility. Thundering footsteps followed, a monstrous twenty-foot tall silver armored automaton pounding past the open doorway.

"Did you see that thing? He wouldn't need any weapons, he could just stomp on us, turn us into pancakes."

"We should go now, before he comes back. If anything happens, hit the violet button on your PIF and run for the elevator."

"The ghost said we go straight across, past all the weapons and vehicles."

They dashed through the door, racing between the long rows of sleek black vehicles and massive beam weapons on circular rolling platforms.

Silas whispered, "Antigrav ships! Lots of them!"

"No time! Run!"

There was another crashing sound from the far side of the cavernous depot.

"He's distracting them! We're good, keep running!"

Two minutes later the breathless group of adventurers reached the far wall.

"Where's the elevator?"

"He said it had bright yellow doors, we couldn't miss it."

"I don't see any yellow doors."

Silas felt sick. The ghost had lied to them. He was right about the ghost being off.

"My bad, wrong wall."

Silas whipped around, his eyes on the ghost's smirking face.

"What did you do?"

The ghost grinned, floating up to the top of a huge metal rack. *"There's been a slight change in plan."*

He held out one hand, a stack of metal pipes sliding toward him, tumbling down to the floor with a horrendous crash.

Silas turned to the others, his eyes wide. "The ghost tricked us! This is the wrong wall!"

Chapter 24

Moving On

"Which way do we go?"

Odo said, "We have two choices, we can go left or go right."

Sephie said, "Go left, the wall is closer. Everyone tap the violet button on your PIF and run for the left wall."

Odo could hear the Guardians pounding across the armory floor toward them.

Emmy slapped her forehead. "So dumb, what was I thinking? You guys go, I'll catch up to you."

Silas said, "We're not leaving you here."

"I'll be fine, I promise. Head for the wall, but go quietly, no talking, no noise."

"What are you going to—"

Emmy floated up above the huge racks, flashing across the room, her eyes on the Guardians. There were four of them. She landed on a rack, converted back to her physical body and grabbed a machine part, pushing it over the edge. She grinned when it hit the floor, the four Guardians stopping and turning.

Emmy hollered, "CATCH ME IF YOU CAN, YOU CRAZY ROBOT!"

She switched to her dream body, shooting across the armory to the far right wall, looking for the elevator doors. There were no yellow elevator doors, which meant the others were headed in the right direction. She landed on a rack, pushing a crate of metal parts over the edge.

"HERE I AM, COME AND GET ME!"

She heard the Guardians thundering down one of the aisles.

"I'M HIDING IN A CRATE, BUT YOU'LL NEVER FIND ME! HA HA HA!"

She floated up, flashing across the room in a split second, spotting the others heading toward the left wall. She soared past them, locating the bright yellow doors. "Gotcha!"

Seconds later she landed next to Sephie, whispering, "Follow me! I found the doors!"

They reached the elevator a minute later, Silas looking for the purple button. "He lied, it's a key pad, not a button, and we don't know the code."

Odo pressed his hand against the elevator, a shimmering translucent doorway appearing. "We don't need a code." He peered into the car. "We're good. Everyone in!"

Silas was about to enter the elevator when he spotted the ghost standing next to one of the racks, a look of stunned disbelief on his face. *"You're leaving me here?"*

There was something about the tone of the ghost's voice that affected Silas in a most unexpected way.

"Come with us. It will be an adventure."

"Come with you? I can't leave this place."

"Sure you can. Come on, it will be fun."

"Why are you doing this? I tried to kill you."

"You watched your friends die here. I understand how angry you are, how sad you are, but it's time to move on. Come with us. We can help you."

The ghost studied Silas' face. *"I can show you how to get out of here. The topside doors take you to a city that was frozen by an Ice Child. So many people died. I lost my family there. All of them."*

"I'm sorry. I can't imagine how awful it must have been for you."

"Four one three four nine eight."

"What's that?"

"The code for the elevator."

"Thank you. Meet us up at the main doors."

"Silas, what are you doing? Hurry up!"

Silas darted into the elevator. Odo was staring at the keypad on the wall. "It needs a code. What do we do? Sephie, is there any way you can bypass the–"

Silas stepped over to the keypad, tapping in the code, the lights blinking on.

The others stared at him. "How did you do that?"

"Lucky guess."

Odo's eyes narrowed.

Emmy slapped the purple glowing tab, the elevator shooting upward.

Ten seconds later the doors slid open, Odo stepping out into the biggest, coldest room he had ever seen.

"It's freezing in here! It must be a billion below zero."

Sephie shaped arctic gear for everyone, the friends pulling on white snow pants and coats.

"Good idea to make them white, it will be hard for anyone to spot us in the snow."

Silas was studying the long black frozen vehicles parked in the gargantuan room. "It's a hangar for military attack ships. They're heavily armored and have crazy weapons."

Odo said, "How do we get out of here?"

The ghost appeared next to Silas, pointing across the room.

Silas said, "That way to the doors."

"How do you know that?"

"I just do."

"You're totally up to something. No way was that elevator code a lucky guess."

Silas smiled. "Fine, it wasn't luck, I just used logic, common sense."

"You used logic to figure out the code? You're so up to something."

The adventurers headed across the massive hangar, reaching the other side ten minutes later, Odo looking up at the titanic doors covered with a thick layer of rock hard ice. "Definitely the biggest doors I've ever seen."

"A hundred feet tall at least."

"How do we open them?"

"We don't." Odo stepped over to one of the doors, pressing his hand against it, peering outside. "It's a city, a big one, tons of skyscrapers. It's frozen, ice everywhere."

The friends stepped through the shimmering doorway into the city, gazing up at the monolithic gleaming buildings.

Silas turned, spotting the ghost.

"You're coming with us?"

"I don't know, I feel different."

"Are you okay? What's wrong?"

"Something is happening. I don't understand."

Silas blinked when he saw a group of glowing white beings appear, surrounding the ghost. He sent a thought to the ghost. *"Who are they?"*

"It's my family, my old friends. They want me to go with them. They had to wait until I was ready."

"Go with them. Thanks for helping us with the code."

The ghost glowed with a brilliant white light. *"I won't forget how you helped me."*

The ghosts vanished.

Emmy was watching Silas. She whispered, "Were you talking to the ghost? What does he want?"

"His family came and got him. It was time for him to

leave this place."

Emmy took Silas' hand.

"He gave me the elevator code. He lost his family when the Ice Child froze the city."

"I'm glad you helped him."

Solis called out, "My medallion is buzzing. I think we're getting close." She turned slowly. "It's pointing to one of those big buildings."

Silas pulled a pair of binoculars from his pack. "Which building?"

"It has a needle shaped tower on top."

Silas peered through the binoculars, scanning the skyscraper.

"There are lights on the top floor, someone is up there. I think we found whoever it is we're supposed to find."

"Who would live at the top of a skyscraper?"

"A wicked witch with an army of flying monkeys?"

Sephie burst out laughing. "That totally makes up for your tectonic plate joke."

Chapter 25

Emergency

The friends headed into the city, stepping cautiously across the jagged cracked slabs of ice. Odo stopped, pointing to one of the shops. "We should go in there and check out all the stuff. They might have some cool high tech gear."

Sephie said, "Go for it."

Odo scrambled across the ice to the shop, scraping the frost off the window and peering in. "Not going in. There are frozen people in there. A lot of them."

"So horrible."

Solis said, "Why do the Children of Ice freeze everyone? I would never do anything like that."

"I think the answer is at the top of that skyscraper."

Silas said, "Odo, climb up the side of the skyscraper and peek in, see who lives there."

Emmy said, "I could fly up and look."

Sephie shook her head. "You don't need to. I don't think the Sinarians would send Solis somewhere dangerous."

Fox appeared next to Solis.

"Dear Fox!" Emmy leaned over and picked him up, cradling him in her arms, Fox resting his head on her shoulder. She listened for a moment, then said, "He wants to be with me when we go up there. He knows I'm afraid of what they might tell me."

Sephie put her hand on Solis' shoulder. "Whatever happens, we're your friends and we'll help you."

"The Sinarian said I would be a savior, but I don't want to be one. I just want to know who I am, where I came from, who my parents are."

"We'll find out. It will be okay, I promise. I didn't know who my parents were until a couple of years ago."

Odo stopped for a moment as they were approaching the skyscraper, gazing up at the colossal structure, eyeing the lights at the top of the building. "All I can say is, this place better have an elevator."

Sephie clapped him on the back. "Think of the great abs you'll have after climbing five hundred flights of stairs."

The adventurers headed for the main doors, Silas peering in through the huge glass windows. "Not good."

"What is it? What do you see?"

"Two heavily armed guards of the scary giant robot variety. It's never a good sign when they have glowing red eyes and black beam weapons."

Odo held up his hand. "Everyone relax, I have a plan. Silas goes in and takes out the robots while we sit out here and eat cookies."

Solis laughed, covering her mouth.

Sephie spotted a violet button next to a circular metal grill. "I think this is an intercom." She pressed a glowing tab, a scratchy voice sounding. "Room number?"

The friends looked at each other. Sephie whispered, "What should I say?"

Silas called out, "Room 1349."

"Thank you. Stand by."

They waited silently for almost a minute.

"What's taking them so long?"

"I don't know." Sephie pressed the button again.

"Room number?"

"It's Room 1349, but we're trying to get in so we can–"

"Thank you. Stand by."

She pressed it again three minutes later.

"Please state the nature of your emergency."

"What emergency?"

"Please state the nature of your emergency."

"I don't have an emergency, we're trying to get up to the top floor so we can talk to–"

"Thank you. Stand by."

They waited for another three minutes, Odo's jaw tightening. He stepped in front of Sephie and pushed the button. "Hello?"

"What is the nature of your emergency?"

"My hair is on fire."

169

"Name please?"

"Little Silas Dingleheimer." Odo hunched over, his hand over his mouth, trying not to laugh out loud.

"Please stand by while we notify the appropriate authorities of your emergency, Little Silas Dingleheimer."

Silas glared at Odo, then shrugged. "It was kind of funny."

Soft music began playing over the speaker.

Four minutes later Odo hit the button again, but the melodious music didn't stop.

"Great, now what? Any ideas?"

"I have one." Solis walked over to the glass doors, rapping on them. One of the robot guards turned slowly, his red eyes pulsing with an eerie light. Solis held her medallion up to the glass, pointing to it.

The robot meandered over to the door, scanning the medallion with a pale green light, his eyes blinking rapidly.

The music stopped, a new voice coming from the speaker. "You may enter the building. The guards will not bother you. I apologize for the confusion."

The glass doors whirred open, the friends stepping into the building, Odo gaping at the colossal atrium. "This place is seriously incredible. Super high tech and fancy."

"We need to find the elevator."

"I'll ask the robots." Odo darted across the foyer. "Can you tell me where the elevator is? We need to get to the top floor."

"Please state the nature of your emergency."

The second robot turned away, snickering.

"What did you say?"

"Please state the nature of your emergency, Little Silas Dingleheimer."

The second robot snorted, slapping his leg.

Odo glared at the robot. "That was you on the speaker?"

"Maybe."

"Start talking or I'll report you to the robot police."

"Down the hall, first left. Have a fantastic day, Little Silas Dingleheimer."

As they headed toward the elevators, Silas whispered, "Those guys were seriously funny. Do you think they were programmed to be funny?"

"They probably have some kind of super advanced engineered intelligence."

Sephie rolled her eyes. "Why would they need super advanced engineered intelligence to play childish pranks like that?"

"Childish? Those jokes were some of the most hilarious–"

Emmy called out, "There's the elevator!"

They approached the gleaming gold doors, pressing the violet disk next to them, a voice sounding.

"Please state the nature of your emergency."

Odo hollered down the hall at the two robots. "Knock

it off, you crazy robots!"

The doors whirred open, the friends stepping into the lift.

Solis was holding Fox close to her, clearly anxious.

Sephie said, "The man on the intercom sounded really nice, not scary at all. We'll be fine."

Odo nodded his agreement, all the while thinking of a dozen possible dreadful scenarios where they would definitely not be fine, including one that involved giant hungry carnivorous insects and a horde of the undead.

Silas pressed the button for the top floor of the building.

"Stay alert, watch out for flying monkeys."

Chapter 26

Noran

The elevator shot upward, Odo's knees almost buckling. They stopped fifteen seconds later, the doors sliding open, an older man with short white hair and sparkling green eyes studying them. He turned to Solis, his face softening.

"You came back."

Solis glanced at Sephie, uncertain what she should say.

"Forgive me, I am Noran. Please come in." He motioned them in, Odo eyeing the long brightly lit room lined with flickering display panels. Silas strolled across the room to a wall of floor-to-ceiling windows, gazing down at the sprawling city two thousand feet below. "We saw your lights from down there. That's how we knew where to go. This view is incredible. Emmy, look how big the city is."

Noran approached Solis, saying, "You don't remember anything, do you?"

Solis shook her head. "Are you my father?"

173

Noran didn't answer her question. "You're here because you want to know who you are and why the medallion brought you to this place?"

"I do."

Fox's piercing eyes were on Noran.

Noran called out, "Ordat!"

A gleaming gold android emerged from a side room. "Sir?"

"Would you mind bringing some snacks to the sitting area for our friends? And some drinks? They've had a long and no doubt very eventful journey."

"Of course. Shall I scan their memories for culinary preferences?"

"No need, just bring a variety of treats."

"Of course."

"Follow me, please." Noran led the friends through a maze of electronic equipment into a luxurious sitting area overlooking the city. "Please, take a seat, make yourselves comfortable."

Odo sank down into a plush green and white striped velvet armchair. "Super comfy chair."

Ordat returned with a large platter of pastries and cookies, stepping over to Silas. "Would you care for a snack, sir?"

"Sure, thanks." Silas took one, nibbling at it. "Yum, these are really good." He grabbed three more.

While Ordat was offering everyone snacks, Noran leaned back, drumming his fingers on the arm of his chair. "A most extraordinary group of travelers indeed. You came all the way from Earth?"

Odo took a cookie from the tray. "We came through a portal."

Solis said, "Odo and Sephie brought me to their time, then to this world. I was living with my mother in a forest long ago. The villagers thought I was a witch because of my hair and eyes."

"That is unfortunate, but not surprising. People fear what is different, unfamiliar."

Noran looked at Sephie. "You are Fortisian?"

"Half Fortisian, half human. My dad was Fortisian, my mom was human, from Earth."

"Interesting."

Solis said, "Who are you? Why did the medallion bring us here?"

Noran gave her a rueful smile. "To be truthful, I didn't think I would ever see you again. I had no choice in the matter, but I wish it had not been so."

"You've seen me before? You know who I am?"

"I have and I do. I was there when the Sinarians took you away. I was the one who asked them to take you to a safe haven, somewhere far from the stark dangers of Suvon."

"Who were my parents? Are they still alive?"

Noran hesitated, then said, "I'm afraid I am the closest thing you have to a parent."

"I don't understand. What happened to my parents?"

"Let me preface my answer by saying that our physical bodies are nothing more and nothing less than organic machines, machines which are inhabited by universal consciousness. Although our consciousness and our physical body are entangled at the quantum level, in the end they are two separate entities. You are not your physical body."

"Sephie can send her consciousness to other places, leaving her body."

"Yes, Fortisians have marvelous powers. Your situation is a little different than most, Solis. Your consciousness is entangled not with an ordinary organic body, but with an impossibly complex bioengineered physical form, one with remarkable capabilities. By that, I mean your ability to manipulate thermal energy."

Solis stared at the old man. "Who were my parents?"

"You did not have parents in the normal sense. We created your body, then entangled it with universal consciousness."

Emmy said, "I'm confused about universal consciousness. What is it?"

"It is impossibly complex, misunderstood by many, fully understood by none, but we do know that consciousness is an integral part of the universe, like the sky, the planets, gravity, the stars, space, dark matter, dark energy. Consciousness and the physical world are one and the same, interconnected, neither capable of existing without the other. It is somewhat like having a dream, your mind and the apparent reality of your dream being one and the same."

Silas said, "You're saying you can entangle universal consciousness with a bioengineered body?"

"It happens every day in nature, on every world inhabited by living beings. Your body is an organic machine controlled by your consciousness. That is nature, part of the universe, part of life as we know it. The worlds are filled with a near infinite variety of physical bodies, those bodies created in a near infinite number of ways. Solis' body happened to be created by scientists."

"I don't have any parents? I'm a machine? I'm a robot?"

"No, you are as alive as I am, as much a living person as your friends are. There is no difference at all between us except for the origin of your physical body. You are life, awareness, consciousness, capable of complex emotions, capable of love, just as we are."

"Who is Fox?"

Noran smiled, his eyes on Fox. "Yes, your dear friend Fox. Are you certain you wish to know the answer to that question?"

Fox looked at Solis. *"It is time."*

"I want to know. It is time."

Fox leaned against her.

"This may be a difficult concept to grasp, but Fox is a spectral being of your own creation. Fox is your deeper self become temporarily incarnate. He is you, a deeper part of you, springing forth from your unconscious mind into this physical world."

"But he's a fox."

"That is the form you unconsciously chose for him. You see him as separate from you now, and you listen to the wisdom of his words, but in time you will merge with him, his thoughts will become your thoughts. You will no longer listen to him, you will be him, and he will be you, your consciousness and awareness expanding."

Emmy said, "That's what happened to me, that's how I learned to fly. I created a dream guide named Nomi. I thought she was separate from me, but she was part of me. We merged, and now we're… just me."

Noran nodded. "Perhaps you can help Solis in her transition. It can be a difficult one."

Odo said, "Who are the Children of Ice? Why are they destroying the world?"

"The Children of Ice are my greatest regret, a colossal and unforgivable error made by myself and a dozen other scientists. They saved our world, but now they are destroying it."

"What are they?"

"They have the same physical body as Solis, with the same powers, but they lack her consciousness, her self awareness, her empathy, her ability to love. They are machines, not living creatures like Solis."

"Why did you make them?"

"There was a war, our world was in chaos. We were

being attacked by Anarkkian interstellar battlecruisers, our weapons not advanced enough to repel them, their energy shields impenetrable. We were being decimated, and they were taking hundreds of prisoners aboard their ships for purposes unknown to us. Our solution was the Children of Ice, virtually indistinguishable from living children, a highly classified project, known only to a handful of people. The plan was to rapidly accelerate their growth cycle, then let them be captured and taken aboard the Anarkkian ships. Once there, they would use their hidden thermal powers to rescue the captives and destroy the ships, either freezing them to absolute zero or absorbing energy from the sun and obliterating them."

"What about Solis?"

"Solis was the first Child of Ice we created, imbued with consciousness, as are many of our androids, but we decided against using her as a weapon because she was a living being with strong innate survival instincts. The Children of Ice who followed her were machines, without consciousness, without awareness. At first, the Ice Child project was a rousing success, hundreds of Suvonians being rescued from the Anarkkian ships, and most of the Anarkkian armada destroyed. They retreated three months later, never to return."

"If the war is over, why are the Children of Ice destroying your world?"

"One of the Anarkkian warships crashed near a facility where the Children of Ice were warehoused, hundreds of them being inadvertently activated. It should not have happened, but it did. We had safeguards, multiple redundant failsafe systems in place, but something happened. We don't know what or why, but it was a disaster of epic proportions, all living creatures within fifty miles of the crash site frozen in less than a day by the Children of Ice.

"Needless to say, the scientists who had created them wanted the Children of Ice neutralized, destroyed. I did not have an issue with destroying the non-living Children of Ice, but I could not bring myself to harm Solis. I had become quite attached to her, and it had been my intention to adopt her, to raise her as my own child. I was outvoted, the other scientists seeing her as a grave threat to Suvon, her powers too great. Before they could destroy her I contacted the Sinarians, asking for their help, giving them my tracker medallion in case she ever decided to return to Suvon. The scientists attempted to neutralize the other Children of Ice, but they failed."

Odo said, "What happens now that Solis is back? Will she stay with you?"

"She needs to live in a community, have friends her own age, not live with a reclusive scientist in an abandoned skyscraper. However, as you are aware, Suvon is currently a very dangerous world. All that being said, I have a solution, one which I hesitate to mention due to the grave dangers involved."

"What is it?"

"I believe that the five of you, working together as a

team, can use your remarkable powers to stop the Children of Ice and end their reign of destruction on Suvon."

Fox spoke to Solis.

"It is why we are here."

Chapter 27

Shotgun!

Odo looked at the others, then at Noran. "You said there were hundreds of them roaming the planet. There's no way we can stop that many. "

"You are quite correct, there are hundreds of them, but there is a way to stop them. The Children of Ice are linked to a central remote deactivation system, a safety protocol developed in the event that we needed to disable them. That is the good news. The bad news is that activating the system will be monumentally difficult. Many have tried, many have failed."

Odo frowned. He didn't like the many have failed part. "What do we have to do? Why is it so hard to activate it?"

"The Ice Children were assembled and warehoused inside a vast, highly secure military complex called Northern Iktar Research & Development Center. When the Anarkkian ship crashed, the main building was severely damaged, all access to the remote system blocked by the wreckage, the upper six levels of the facility completely destroyed by the starship. We think the Children of Ice escaped from a secondary storage facility in the complex, which was also damaged, but we have no idea how they were activated. Two undamaged storage bunkers still hold over three hundred deactivated Children of Ice."

"Where is the remote deactivation mechanism?"

"On the seventh sublevel of the central HQ building, beneath the crashed Anarkkian starship."

Emmy said, "Why is it so dangerous? Can't they just dig through the rubble and find a way down to the seventh level?"

"There are five or six Children of Ice roaming the complex, and the sublevels are protected by Guardians, extremely powerful heavily armored automatons, all placed on high alert when the Anarkkian ship crashed."

"We saw four Guardians in an underground military armory. They almost killed us but we managed to escape by tricking them."

Silas added, "A ghost gave me the passcode to unlock the elevators."

Odo spun around. "That crazy ghost who tried to kill us? Why were you talking to him?"

"He turned out to be okay. He lost his family and his friends to the Children of Ice, and then lost his own life. He went a little crazy."

"Oh. You helped him move on?"

"That's why he gave us the code. When he left the

armory his family came for him. He went with them, but he gave me the elevator code before he left."

Sephie said, "Is there any way to stop the Guardians?"

"None that I am aware of, but before you confront them, you must contend with the Children of Ice roaming the complex. They can freeze you to absolute zero in less than thirty seconds."

"Where is the facility? Is it far from here?"

"Four hundred miles from here, but I can help you with transportation. I have two military scout ships parked on the level below us."

"Scout ships?"

"They are armed antigrav vehicles large enough to hold all of you."

Odo called out, "Dibs on pilot seat!"

Silas hollered, "Shotgun!"

Sephie looked at Emmy, shaking her head.

Solis said, "What is an antigrav vehicle?"

"Remember the cars you saw driving around Bedford Falls? They're kind of like that, but they can fly."

"They can fly? Will you teach me to fly it?"

Sephie laughed. "Absolutely."

Noran said, "I have beam weapons, if that would help. They would prove useless against the Guardians or the Children of Ice, but there are gangs of bandits roaming the cities. It's chaos out there."

"Thanks, but we won't need them."

Silas said, "There is one thing you could help us

with."

"Name it."

"Those snacks we had? Maybe we could get a box of the ones with the orange berries?"

Odo nodded. "And some of the star shaped ones, they were really good too."

"I will have Ordat prepare several boxes for you."

Noran pulled a small round disk from his coat pocket. "This nav disk will guide you to the R&D Center. I've marked its location and plotted a relatively safe course for you, one that bypasses the major cities. You should know that during the Anarkkian invasion, thousands of autonomous ground to air defense weapons were installed across our world, but most could not be deactivated, thanks to the Children of Ice. An alarm in the scout ship will sound if a weapon locks onto you. Fly low, at treetop level, and you should be able to avoid them. If the alarm sounds, you must land the ship immediately, do not hesitate. Press the yellow button on the main console to activate the emergency landing sequence."

Solis turned to Noran. "What happens if we do manage to stop the Children of Ice?"

"Come back here and I will find us a safe place to live, a community where you will have friends your age. You can tell them I am your father, if that would make things easier for you. Our world will begin again, our lives will begin again."

Solis said, "I would like that. It would be nice if there was a forest."

Sephie was gazing out the window at the setting suns. "Can we stay here tonight and leave in the morning?"

"Of course, I will have Ordat prepare dinner for us. After that, we can go down to the hangar and I will familiarize you with the controls of the scout ship. You have flown antigrav ships before?"

"We have, on several worlds."

"Excellent. They're really quite simple to operate. Oh, take this and keep it with you at all times; it's a tracker so I'll know where you are, know if you need help."

The following morning the adventurers rose with the sun, had a quick breakfast, then took the elevator down to the hangar. Odo grinned, rubbing his hands together, stopping short when he saw Sephie jump into the pilot seat.

"What are you doing? I called dibs on being the pilot."

"That was yesterday, this is today. You snooze, you lose."

Emmy laughed. "We can take turns flying."

"Fine." Odo tossed his backpack into the ship, climbing in, stretching out on a padded passenger seat. "Comfy. The seats even recline."

Noran stepped over to Solis, putting his hand on her shoulder. "Please be careful."

"I will."

186

Sephie said, "Solis, you take the copilot seat and I'll teach you how to fly this thing. It's not hard."

Noran pressed a button on the wall and the hangar doors rolled open, a cold wind rushing into the room. "Good luck to you all."

Sephie tapped two tabs on the console, the control lights blinking on, then inched the stick back, the ship rising a few feet above the floor. She closed the glass canopy, waving to Noran as the ship flew out through the open hangar doors.

She pulled the nav disk from her pocket, handing it to Solis. "Drop this into that slot and push the violet tab next to it."

A holographic map blinked up in front of them, a glowing blue line marking their path.

"Okay, that red dot is us; we just follow the blue line for four hundred miles."

"Don't forget to fly low."

"I set it for one hundred feet above ground level, and activated the three dimensional obstacle avoidance. We're good to go." She tapped a button, the ship descending to one hundred feet, autonomously weaving around the skyscrapers as it shot through the city.

Chapter 28

Old Nokti

Odo woke, rubbing his eyes. "What's happening? Why is the ship shaking? Why is it dark out?"

"Another big storm, a bad one. We have to land."

Odo turned, eyeing the massive wall of black storm clouds heading toward them, brilliant flashes of lightning punctuated by deafening crashes of thunder. "That thing is crazy! Take us down before it hits us."

"We're over a city, it could be dangerous, maybe bandits."

A massive gust of wind grabbed the ship, rocking it wildly, a box of snacks spilling onto the floor. "My snacks!"

"We're landing, bandits or no bandits!"

Sephie slapped the yellow emergency button, the ship plummeting downward, Odo letting out a screech.

Seconds later their descent slowed, the adventurers pressed down into their seats, the craft hovering a few feet above a wide boulevard.

Silas hollered, "Over there, through those big doors!

It looks like a parking garage!"

Sephie turned the ship, shooting toward the massive glass and steel structure.

They flashed through the entryway just as a deluge of rain hit, the streets turning to rivers, churning black thunderclouds enveloping the city in a veil of darkness.

Sephie flipped on the ship's lights. "It's not a parking garage, it's an entrance to something, maybe a transport station."

The ship landed with a gentle thump.

Odo leaned back in his seat. "So we just sit here and wait until the storm is over?"

"I guess so. It probably won't last too long."

Sephie said, "We could poke around, see if we find anything cool."

Odo nodded. "Like a cool gang of bandits who want to kill us?"

"Do you see any bandits? They might have shops here, maybe some nice clothes."

Odo grabbed his pack. "Or shops filled with gold coins and jewels."

"HELP ME! PLEASE!"

The friends turned, their eyes on an old man in ragged clothes staggering out of a darkened doorway. He stumbled toward them. "It's my daughter, she's trapped down below and it's flooding! I can't get the door open. She'll drown if we don't get her out!"

"Where is she?"

The adventurers piled out of the ship, the man holding his leg. "I hurt my leg, it might be broken, I can't get to her. She's two floors down, you'll have to take the stairs. The water's bad, I've never seen a storm like this, it's flooding fast."

Odo headed through the doorway, Sephie shaping a sphere of bright light to illuminate the corridor, the others right behind them.

Silas called out, "Take those stairs!" They raced down the steps two at a time, reaching the floor below them.

"One more level down!"

Solis called out, "I can freeze the water, stop the flooding!"

"Good idea!"

"He said she's down here. Which way?"

Sephie stopped, her eyes narrowing. "I don't hear any water."

"I don't either. I think this is a train station. Look at all the gates."

Odo called out, "Hello? Is anyone here?"

"Where is she? There's no water down here, no flooding."

Emmy said, "We need to go back up. Now!"

"That guy tricked us!"

They raced back up the stairs, darting through the doorway into the foyer, Odo stopping short.

"Our ship is gone! That guy took it! He stole our ship."

"All our stuff was in it, our backpacks, everything."

"He took my orange berry snacks!"

Emmy turned to Silas. "What?"

"He took my snacks, the ones with the orange berries. I only had one box of them left, I was saving them for later."

Sephie peered outside at the monstrous storm, torrents of rain pounding the streets. "It's not slowing down at all."

"I can't believe he took the ship out in that storm."

Silas flopped down on one of the long benches lining the wall. "We still have at least a hundred miles to go."

"We can look around for another vehicle once the storm dies down."

Odo gave a yelp. "What is that?"

The friends turned, staring at three leafy visitors who had darted inside, watching them shake the water from their branches.

Emmy whispered, "Walking trees, like the ones at the orchard."

"Oh, great, we're going to get eaten by trees."

One of the trees turned toward the adventurers.

Silas whispered, "It's looking at us. I think."

"How about this weather? It's wild out there, isn't it? These storms just keep getting worse."

Odo whispered, "Did anyone else hear that?"

They all nodded, their eyes on the trees.

Solis sent a thought back to them. *"It's really bad.*

How much longer do you think it will last?"

The tree shrugged. *"No way to tell, really. Could be hours, could be days, could be weeks. Everything is frozen solid ten miles east of here. A Child of Ice is passing through."*

"Someone stole our ship, he said his daughter was trapped down below."

"Oh, that was crazy old Nokti. He's a lunatic and a legend."

"You know him?"

"Everyone knows him. You're not the first one to fall for his tricks. He takes the ships for a ride then dumps them. You can use your tracker to find it after the storm dies down."

"We don't have a tracker."

"Oh, that's not good. Where are you headed?"

"We're trying to get to the Northern Iktar Research & Development Center."

"You can take a train, I think they're still running. The A14 Express will take you to Iktar. Or you can wait till the storm is over and look for your ship. Old Nokti probably didn't go too far in this weather."

"Thanks, we might do that."

Odo sent out a thought. *"Do all the trees walk on Suvon?"*

"What do you mean?"

"In our world, trees don't walk, they have roots that grow into the ground and they just stay in one spot."

"Oh, young ones don't walk, just the adults. It would be dreadful to spend your whole life rooted."

One of the trees rustled its branches. *"We should get going or we'll be late."*

"Good luck finding your ship."

"Thanks. See you."

Odo plopped back down on the bench. "They seemed nice enough, you know, for talking trees. Do they have faces? I wasn't sure where to look when I talked to him."

Silas had a dark expression. "I hope Nokti closed the canopy so my snacks don't get soggy.".

Chapter 29

Protect the Others

After a leisurely lunch and some stories for Solis about their recent adventures in Pangaea, the storm outside was still raging, the wind howling.

Sephie said, "I guess we should try to take the train. The trees said the storm could last for weeks, and we have no way to track the scout ship."

"Do you really want to go down in some creepy abandoned train station? Who knows what's down there, it could be crawling with hordes of the undead."

The color drained from Solis' face. "What are the undead? That sounds very scary."

Sephie said, "The undead are very scary, but the good news is they only exist in Odo's imagination."

Emmy stood up. "I like trains, they're fun. Let's go."

The adventurers headed down the stairs, Sephie sending a bright orb of light ahead of them.

They reached the long row of gates, studying the signs. "The tree said we should take the A14 Express?"

"That one, right there." Silas pointed to one of the

gates.

"How can you read that?"

Silas tapped the gold disk on his temple. "Translator disk?"

"Oh, right." Odo grabbed a translator disk from his pack, pressing it to his forehead.

They walked through the gate, Silas saying, "We take those stairs."

"The lights are on down there. Nice."

The friends took a seat on a long row of metal benches, Odo peering down the murky tunnel. "The good news is, no hordes of the undead. The bad news is, no train."

"Relax, it will be here soon."

Fifteen minutes later a voice boomed out across the station.

"A14 Express arriving in one minute. Final stop, Northern Iktar Research & Development Center."

"Perfect, that's where we want to go. This is great."

Fox appeared on the bench next to Solis. She grinned, scratching his ears. *"My old friend Fox."*

"You must move quickly once it begins. Head to the surface, protect the others. Keep your eyes on the sky."

"Once what begins? What's going to happen?"

Fox vanished.

"What did Fox want?"

"He said we have to move quickly once it begins, but he didn't say what. He said to head for the surface and keep our eyes on the sky."

"What does that mean?"

Sephie said, "I'm pretty sure it means the train won't be taking us to the R&D Center."

A rush of wind hit them as the A14 train shot out of the tunnel, coming to a stop in front of them, the doors whirring open.

"Final stop, Northern Iktar Research & Development Center. All aboard!"

"What do we do?"

"We take the train and be ready for anything."

The friends scrambled onto the car, taking their seats. "Soft chairs. Comfy."

The doors hissed shut, the train shooting forward.

Ten minutes passed, Odo's initial anxiety about Fox's cryptic message diminishing. "Maybe Fox was just telling us to be careful, you know, to keep our eyes open, just in case."

Emmy shivered. "Is it getting cold?"

Solis said. "It's not me."

"Look, frost on the windows!"

"What do we do?"

Sephie shaped her Varanian arctic gear as quickly as she good, passing it out to everyone. "Put this on. Hurry!"

"Fox said to head for the surface as soon as it begins."

Silas stood up, darting over to a glass box on the wall. "Hold on!" He flipped up the glass cover, pressing the yellow button, the train squealing to a halt, almost knocking him over.

Emmy said, "How do we open the doors?"

"We don't." Odo pressed his hand against the door, a shimmering exit appearing. "Everyone out!"

The group of friends scrambled out the door, Odo glancing at the train car. "Hey, there's no wheels on the train, it must be a mag lev or maybe an anti-grav–"

"Focus, Odo. We have to find a way up to the surface."

Silas called out, "Emergency exit down there!"

"It's getting colder!"

They reached the exit, pulling open a heavy metal door.

"Up these stairs! We have to hurry."

"Fox said to keep our eyes on the sky."

They raced up four flights of stairs, emerging outside in a small covered waiting area, scanning their surroundings.

"It's a little town. It looks empty."

"It's freezing, everything is covered with ice and snow."

Sephie gave a shout. "Over there! Look!"

Odo spotted the young girl with green eyes and white hair. "She looks like Solis."

Silas whispered, "It's an Ice Child!"

The white haired girl turned slowly, looking up at the sky, holding out both arms. There was a crackling sound, the temperature dropping rapidly. Sephie shaped a powerful sphere of energy around them. "This will help."

"How do we stop her?"

Solis was remembering Fox's words, *protect the others*. She stepped forward. "Wait here."

"What are you doing?"

Solis gazed up at the sky, facing the two suns. She held out both arms, her body flaring brightly. The Child of Ice turned, staring at her.

"What's it doing?"

"I think it's attracted to the bright light and heat, to thermal energy."

Solis lowered her arms, her open palms facing the Child of Ice. A raging storm of blinding white hot light flashed out, hitting the Child of Ice. Solis lowered her arms, her eyes on the green-eyed bioform, now glowing with a blazing white light, the ice around her melting.

Odo whispered, "Did Solis stop her?"

Emmy looked up when she heard the humming sound, spotting two silver antigrav ships high above them. One of them fired a sizzling stream of incandescent orange light at the Child of Ice.

"Cover your eyes!"

The Child of Ice erupted in a ball of radiant white hot light, meandering away from the adventurers. The second silver ship fired, the Child of Ice again looking skyward. A titanic pillar of flaming light shot up, vaporizing one of the ships, the green-eyed Child of Ice visible again. She raised both arms, waves of thermal energy streaming down from the second ship.

"She's freezing the ship, taking all its thermal energy! We have to stop her!"

Solis was turning toward the sun when she saw a second Child of Ice ambling toward them.

"There's two of them! I can't fight two of them!"

The silver scout ship was descending rapidly, landing with a loud thump fifty feet away from them.

Solis cried out, "Run for the ship while I hold them off!"

She held out her arms, draining the thermal energy from the nearest Child of Ice. It slowed down, looking confused for a moment, then stared up at the sun.

"Hurry!"

Odo reached the ship, peering through the glass canopy. "They're frozen! There are two frozen dead guys!"

Sephie hollered, "Pull them out, we need the ship!"

"They're dead, frozen. I'm not going to–"

Silas ran past Odo, raising the canopy. "Help me, Odo!"

Odo groaned, helping Silas drag the two frozen bodies from the ship. "Dead guys, I'm touching dead guys."

"No time for that! Hurry, get in! Solis! Let's go!"

They piled into the antigrav ship, Odo mashing the buttons. "What's wrong with this thing?" He pressed a small yellow button and the ship blasted up into the air, flashing across the city.

"We did it!" Odo grabbed the stick, pulling it back, then pushing it forward, fear washing over his face. "I can't steer it! It's flying by itself!"

Chapter 30

Waiting

"Which buttons did you push?"

"I pushed a lot of them, but nothing happened until I hit the yellow one. I was kind of in a hurry."

"No one's blaming you, but we have to deactivate the autopilot."

Odo and Sephie studied the controls, pushing every combination of buttons and dials and tabs they could think of, with no luck.

"It's not working, I still can't steer it."

"The yellow button must have activated an autonomous return home function."

"I guess we just wait. I wish I knew where home was."

Silas called out, "We're flying over a city."

"How far are we from North Iktar?"

"No idea, but we're going in the wrong direction. We're heading west, not north, traveling about eighty miles an hour."

"We're going down!"

Silas studied the huge complex below them. "It looks

like a transport center, check out those giant interstellar ships. Those things are huge."

Odo said, "It must be a military base. The smaller ships are armed with some serious weapons."

The ship landed in front of a long dark blue building, three uniformed soldiers running out, waving to them.

Odo opened the canopy and stood up, one of the soldiers pulling a vicious looking black weapon from his holster, aiming it at Odo. "Identify yourself!"

"I'm Odo Whitley, and these are my friends Sephie, Silas, Emmy, and Solis. We're lost. What is this place?"

A second soldier pulled out his weapon when Solis stood up. "ICE CHILD!"

Sephie waved her arms, hollering, "She's not an Ice Child! She just looks like one. She's our friend. She won't hurt you!"

"Where's our crew? Where's the other ship?"

Sephie climbed out of the ship, approaching the soldiers. "Your ships were attacked by two Children of Ice. There weren't any survivors. An Ice Child froze this ship and it landed near us. We managed to get it flying, barely escaping with our lives, but we couldn't steer it. It brought us here."

"I told them it was too dangerous. I shouldn't have let them go. I told them."

"I'm sorry."

The soldier studied Sephie's face. "Who are you? Where are you from? You're not from Suvon, not with hair like that."

"We're from Earth. We were on our way to the Northern Iktar Research & Development Center when the two Children of Ice attacked us, freezing everything. Your two ships attacked them, probably trying to help us."

"Why are you going to the Iktar base?"

"We're going to shut down the Children of Ice with the remote deactivation system."

"Suicide. You'll be killed, just like everyone else who's tried to stop them."

"We talked to a scientist who used to work there. We know what to do, we can shut them down."

"You'll be killed. The place is crawling with Children of Ice and Guardians."

Emmy floated up off the ground. "We have powers."

The soldier took a step back. "Who are you, exactly?"

Silas said, "We're the Odd Squad. We save worlds."

Odo eyed Silas, but said nothing.

Emmy said, "It's true, we do. We all have powers."

Silas added, "We could use your help though. We know the Iktar complex has six or seven Children of Ice roaming around, but I think we can distract them long enough to find a way down into the sublevels. The remote deactivation system is located on the seventh sublevel."

"Distract them? How?"

"With thermal weapons. The Children of Ice are attracted to heat and bright light, they feed off it."

"We have plasma bombs, there's nothing hotter. We've tried them before, but the Children of Ice just absorb the heat."

"We're not trying to destroy them, just distract them, get them away from the base. If you drop a bunch of plasma bombs a mile or two away from the main building, it will draw them away long enough for us to find a way down."

"We can do that. We have seven scout ships left. Each one can carry two plasma bombs."

"Can you fly us to Iktar?"

"I can get you within a mile of the base, but you're on your own after that. Any closer and the Children of Ice will take our ship down. How will you get down into the sublevels?"

"I can walk through walls."

The soldier looked less than convinced. "Really?"

Solis said, "I've seen him do it many times."

Odo pressed his hand against the ship, a rippling translucent circle appearing. He pushed his arm through the hull and pulled it out again.

"Okay, I believe you. We'll do whatever we can to help you. Let's head inside and make our plans. You can stay here tonight and we'll leave for Iktar at sunrise. I'm Captain Eli, by the way. I'm in charge of this base, or at least what's left of it."

Silas was eyeing a group of ghosts standing near the main doors. One of them waved to him. He turned to

Emmy, saying, "You guys go in, I'll catch up to you."

She whispered, "You see ghosts?"

"A bunch of them wearing military uniforms. They're looking at me, one of them waved."

Silas made his way over to the group of ghosts, sending them a thought. *"Hi, I'm Silas. How come you guys are still here?"*

"You're trying to get to the remote deactivation system? Knock out the Children of Ice?"

"We are. Someone told us an Anarkkian ship had crashed onto the main building?"

"They were right, I've seen it, I was there. We were part of a team trying to get into the base. We managed to avoid the Children of Ice and we found a way through the crashed Anarkkian ship down to the third sublevel. That's when we ran into a Guardian. He got all of us. We never had a chance, our energy beams just bounced off him."

"I'm sorry, it must have been awful."

"It was quick."

"You said you went down through the Anarkkian ship?"

"It's an easy way to get down, no digging. We were lucky, stumbled onto it. Maybe lucky isn't the right word. There's a big hole in the hull on the east side of the ship. Go in there, head down four decks and you'll find a tear in the hull that opens into the third sublevel of the HQ. I remember seeing a bunch of orange machines near the

opening."

"How come you're still here? You haven't moved on."

"We've been waiting for you. Waiting to tell you about the passageway down through the Anarkkian ship."

"Who told you we were coming?"

The ghost didn't answer Silas' question. *"Do what we couldn't do, shut down the Children of Ice."*

"We will, I promise you."

"Good luck. Time for us to go."

Silas watched the group of ghosts flare brightly and vanish. He turned and walked into the building. Emmy was waiting for him.

"What happened? What did the ghosts say?"

"They told me how to get down to the third sublevel of the main building. They were all killed by a Guardian down there."

"That's so sad."

"They stayed behind because they knew we were coming. They wanted to help us, tell us how to get down there."

"How did they know we were coming? Who told them?"

"They wouldn't say."

Chapter 31

The Blue Button

"It's not dumb, it would look super cool. Watch, I'll show you." Silas climbed up onto a chair, then jumped off, landing with one knee touching the floor, fists clenched, one in front of him, one behind him, his head at an odd angle.

"I still don't get it. What are you doing?"

"It's a cool superhero pose for when you jump off something and land."

"Why?"

"Because it looks totally cool; you're like a coiled spring, ready to leap into action. We should all do it."

Odo glanced at Sephie.

Sephie said, "You're saying Emmy would have to do that every time she lands? It seems like it would be bad for your knees."

Odo nodded. "Really bad. Besides, I don't need to be a coiled spring ready to leap into action. All I do is walk through walls."

Silas glared at him. "No secret handshake, and now

no cool superhero poses? We're the Odd Squad, we should be doing stuff like this, have some signature moves that people will recognize."

Odo groaned. "Fine, we can have a secret handshake, but I'm not doing those weird superhero poses. They look ridiculous."

Silas grinned, holding his open hand out to Emmy. She slapped a five dollar bill into his palm.

"What's that for? Why are you giving him five dollars?"

Silas grinned. "Just a little bet we had. I've been thinking about the secret handshake. It should be complicated, hard to follow, but short, succinct, only last three or four seconds at the most. We can have an abbreviated version for time sensitive occasions, like if we're in the middle of a battle with alien robots or something. It would be like a secret Odd Squad high five."

Odo stared at Silas. "You are so deranged. Wait, were those superhero poses a trick to get your secret handshake? Is that why Emmy gave you the five dollars?"

"A very successful trick."

Sephie burst out laughing. "I like it, let's have a secret handshake."

The friends were interrupted by a knock on the door. "Breakfast!"

"Okay, thanks!" They exited the room, heading down a long corridor to the bustling mess hall, the tables full of Suvonian soldiers, a dozen or so standing in line to get their food.

Twenty minutes later they were eating breakfast, Odo looking up when Captain Eli entered the room.

"Good morning, everyone. I hope you're all rested. It's going to be a busy day. They're loading the plasma bombs as we speak. Flight time is about an hour, fly low and slow to avoid any operational autonomous defense weapons. We'll be dropping the Odd Squad a mile from the R&D Center."

He stepped over to Odo, handing him a small rectangular object. "When you're ready, press the blue button and we'll drop the thermal bombs at least a mile away from the main HQ. The Children of Ice will definitely know we dropped them."

A soldier approached Captain Eli, whispering something to him. Captain Eli nodded. "Excellent, bring them in." He turned to the adventurers with a smile. "I have something that might interest you."

Two soldiers stepped into the room carrying five backpacks and a box.

Odo jumped up from the table. "Our backpacks! Where did you find them?"

"We received a coded message from someone named Noran, saying his scout ship had returned with your backpacks. He's been tracking your posistion, knew where you were. We sent a ship last night to pick up your gear."

Silas flipped open the box, grinning. "The snacks

didn't get wet. I'll bring them with us."

Captain Eli said, "Are you ready?"

Odo was about to say he was born ready, but decided against it. Captain Eli did not look like someone who would appreciate a hilarious and ironic catch phrase. "Ready."

The friends headed outside to the concrete landing pad, Silas eyeing the seven gleaming black scout ships with blinking yellow lights, a chorus of low humming sounds filling the air. "Those ships are so cool."

Captain Eli led them over to a scout ship. "You'll ride in this one, no plasma bombs in it. Don't forget, once you're in position, push the blue button and we drop the plasma bombs. You're on your own after that."

"We need to be dropped on the east side of the crashed Anarkkian ship."

"Your call, we'll drop you wherever you want."

They hopped into the ship, taking their seats. The pilot turned to them. "We're good to go? You have everything you need?"

"Good to go."

"Okay, low and slow, avoiding the cities. We'll be landing one mile east of the Anarkkian wreckage. Push the blue the button when you're in position."

Silas whispered, "Odo, don't forget to push the blue button when we're in position."

"You're deranged."

Silas snickered.

"Here we go." The humming grew louder, all seven scout ships lifting off, heading toward the North Iktar Research & Development Center.

The friends looked down over the side of the ship as they flew above the countryside. Emmy called out, "Walking trees on our left, a big group of them."

"So cool. We should take a little one back to Mrs. Beasley for the flower show. Gold medal for sure."

"They're sentient beings, not plants. You'd be stealing someone's little kid."

"Good point. Look at those guys walking through that village. They look like bandits, they're all carrying weapons."

Odo was studying a large cluster of floating translucent vine orbs when the pilot called out, "Sealing canopy! Ice Child ahead, temperature dropping. I'll crank up the heat."

They flashed over the frigid frozen ground, the trees covered with ice, frost rapidly forming on the ship's canopy. Two minutes later the pilot said, "All clear, past the freeze zone."

Silas was eating one of the orange berry snacks when the ship began to slow down, the pilot calling out, "ETA is four minutes. Get your gear together, this is going to be quick. I don't want to hang around this place, too many Ice Children."

The friends slung their packs on, studying the dense forest below. "I can't tell if they're walking trees or not.

No sign of bandits though."

"We're here, I'll drop you in that clearing. Head west for a mile and you'll hit the Anarkkian ship. Good luck to you. Don't forget to push the blue button when you're in position."

"Got it, press the blue button." Silas nudged Odo, grinning.

The ship descended rapidly, landing gently on the spongy forest floor. "Everyone out!"

The pilot raised the glass canopy, the friends jumping out of the ship. Odo gave the pilot a thumbs up sign and the ship rose up, streaking off above the treetops.

They stepped into the shadowy forest, scanning it for dangerous creatures. "No crazy vine orbs, no hordes of undead. None of the trees are walking, they must be young ones."

"We head west. It shouldn't take us long, it's just a mile. Silas, I forget what we're supposed to do when we're in position. Do you remember what it was?"

"Umm… let me think… we had to press something, a green button maybe?"

"I think it was a yellow button."

"Or was it red?"

Sephie punched Odo's arm. "Let's go, lunatic."

Silas laughed as they headed through the forest.

Solis was the first to spot the crashed Anarkkian ship.

Odo peered through the trees, gaping at the titanic craft. "It's gigantic!"

212

Chapter 32

The Guardian

Silas studied the massive alien ship. "It's bigger than an aircraft carrier."

"Way bigger, probably twice as big. That's crazy. Where do we go in?"

Silas pulled out his binoculars, scanning the wreckage. "About a hundred feet from the stern of the ship, there's a big hole. It looks like it got blown out from the inside, probably a thermal beam from an Ice Child. That's our way in. We'll have to do a little climbing, but it won't be too bad."

"Is everyone ready?"

"Let's do it."

"Odo, would you like to do the honors?"

Odo took out Captain Eli's rectangular communication device.

Emmy whispered, "Over there, an Ice Child!"

"Do it, Odo."

Odo pressed the blue button.

"It's heading this way!"

The sky to the west suddenly turned a bright yellow orange color, the ground shaking, a low thundering roar rolling past them.

The approaching Ice Child stopped, turning toward the brilliant orange glow.

"Look at the sky, it's all wavy from the heat."

"They're leaving. It's working!"

"Let's go."

The adventurers darted out of the forest, running toward the titanic ship. "Over that way, we can climb up that big pile of rubble. Hurry!"

The friends scrambled up the twisted mound of steel beams and concrete, stopping at the top.

"There's the opening, but how do we get up there?"

Emmy said, "I'll fly us up. Sephie, shape a rope and we'll use it to pull Solis up."

"Got it. Solis, wait here and we'll throw a rope down for you."

Ten minutes later the five adventurers were climbing through the gaping hole into the monstrous Anarkkian battlecruiser, Sephie shaping a bright orb of light.

Odo looked around the twisted deck, frowning. "So many skeletons. I hate skeletons."

Emmy said, "Look how big they are."

"Silas, which way do we go?"

"We go down three more levels and look for a bunch of orange machinery. There's a tear in the ship there that opens up to the third sublevel of the research center."

"Look for some stairs, or an elevator."

"This place is a maze. What's with all these crazy corridors?"

"Over there, an arrow pointing down with a bunch of symbols next to it!"

"Nice."

They ran to the sign, Odo sliding open a tall door. "It's not made out of metal, it's some kind of synthetic material."

Silas was about to reply when they heard a loud clanking, scraping noise coming from behind them.

"What's that noise? Is it a Guardian?"

"Don't want to know. Let's go!"

They darted into the stairwell, closing the door behind them, racing down the stairs, Sephie sending out another orb of light.

"No more stairs, we have to find another way down."

They wandered through the maze of corridors, Odo stopping to peer through a smashed window into a partially lit room. "What is that stuff?"

"It looks like weapons and armor."

"We should get some armor. That would be kind of cool."

"Did you see how big those skeletons were? No way would it fit us."

"What about a cool beam weapon?"

"We're on a stealth mission, Odo. Beam weapons won't stop a Guardian."

"Hey, Odo, that room over there is filled with piles of gold coins."

"Ha ha."

"There's another one of those arrows pointing down!"

They raced down the corridor, sliding the door open, peering into the stairwell. "All clear, no undead."

They crept down the stairs, emerging into a cavernous room, the battered floor sloping downward at a steep angle. "What is this?"

"It's a hangar, badly damaged in the crash. Check out all the mangled scout ships piled up at that end."

"They're all charred, there must have been a big fire."

"What does that skeleton have on his back?"

"I'm not sure, it could be an antigrav pack though."

"How cool is that? We should take it."

"You're going to steal something from a creepy dead skeleton?"

Odo hesitated, eyeing the twisted bones of the skeleton. "It's not exactly stealing, but the pack looks kind of big. It probably wouldn't fit me anyway."

"Right."

It took them another half hour to find their way down to the fourth deck level, Emmy spotting a long row of orange machines at the end of a wide corridor. "You said orange machines, right?"

Silas nodded. "There it is, that whole section of the hull is torn open. That's how we get into the sublevels. This is the dangerous part, so be careful. This is where the ghosts were killed by a Guardian."

"What do we do if we see one?"

Sephie said, "I'll shape us some PIFs. Don't forget, push the purple tab to activate the invisibility field. It will last for five minutes."

"They worked great at the armory when the Guardians were chasing us."

"I wish there was some way to disable the Guardians."

Silas said, "Solis, do you think you could freeze one? If they get cold enough they won't be able to move, and it might even damage their electronics, fry their engineered intelligence."

"I can try, I've been practicing and I'm getting close to absolute zero."

"The ones at the armory survived the big freeze."

"It might work if it's a direct thermal attack focused on one Guardian, if I absorb all its energy."

Sephie set her pack down. "I'll scout out the sublevel with the Traveling Eye, see if there are still Guardians here."

She took a seat on the floor, closing her eyes, allowing her consciousness to leave her body, drifting down through the tear in the ship's hull. Her heart sank when she saw it, a huge silver Guardian standing motionless behind a long metal counter, its eyes glowing with a 3dull red light. A sick feeling rolled through her when she saw the seven humanoid skeletons lying in the corridor. "Those must be Silas' ghost friends. They walked right into this." She floated back to her body, her eyes opening.

"That was quick."

"There's a Guardian right as you go in, he's standing behind a counter. There were seven skeletons on the floor."

Silas frowned. "That's where they all died. They warned me about the Guardian there."

"They saved our lives."

Solis said, "I think I can freeze it. I can wear a PIF, climb down there and absorb the Guardian's thermal energy before he knows what's happening. Once he's frozen, maybe we can permanently disable him."

"You're sure you want to do it? It's really dangerous."

"Fox said it's why I'm here. He thinks the Sinarians knew this was going to happen."

"They did say you would save a world."

Solis snapped the PIF onto her wrist, gingerly climbing in through the ragged tear in the hull. She took a deep breath, letting it out slowly. "I can do this, I know I can. It's why the Sinarians chose me."

She tapped the purple tab on her PIF. "Okay, no noise, just like I'm back in the forest." Solis dropped down onto the corridor floor, landing silently, motionless, holding her breath. She studied the monstrous Guardian standing behind the counter, hearing Fox's voice in her head.

"We are one."

218

Chapter 33

Sephie's Appointment

Solis took a deep, slow breath, her eyes on the Guardian. This had to be quick, she couldn't give it any time to react. She felt the power building up inside her, waves of energy rippling through her.

In less than a second Solis was transformed into a blinding ball of white hot light, absorbing the Guardian's energy. She watched the Guardian tumble over in slow motion, hitting the floor with a tremendous crash, the deck shaking, the robot frozen to near absolute zero. She had taken all the energy from its power source, its neural pathways shutting down in less than a second. She turned when she heard footsteps thundering down the hallway toward her.

"INTRUDER!"

The Guardian's red eyes were blazing as it extended one arm, its fist glowing with a brilliant purple light. The Guardian was fast, but Solis was faster, a blazing stream of incandescent plasma hitting the Guardian, instantly vaporizing the top half of him. Solis staggered backwards, her world turning black. She reached out, grabbing at the counter, sliding to the floor, her eyes closed, her body motionless.

Odo and Sephie dropped down from the upper deck, Sephie crying out, "Something happened to Solis!"

Sephie ran over to her, kneeling down next to her. "She's breathing. I think she's okay."

"Did the Guardian hurt her?"

"I don't think so. She took out two of them. The top half of that one is gone."

"Whoa."

Sephie gently shook Solis' shoulder. "Solis? Are you okay?"

Her eyes opened. "I did it, I stopped two of them. I must have fainted. I don't know why."

Sephie helped Solis to her feet. "You're feeling better?"

"I feel fine now. It was too much, too fast. I think I sent out too much of my own energy, but it worked. I used the thermal energy from the first Guardian to destroy the second one."

Emmy said, "You were amazing. It's why the Sinarians wanted you here. No one else could have done this. No one."

Silas said, "You're officially a member of the Odd Squad now, so you can help us work on our secret handshake. It has to be something that–"

Emmy whispered, "Silas, not exactly the time to be

working on our secret handshake."

"May I help you?"

The friends whipped around, Odo giving a screech when he saw the huge Guardian standing behind the counter, one of its eyes blinking with a bright yellow light. It spoke again.

"May I help you?"

Odo's eyes were wide. "What?"

"May I help you? Do you have an appointment, or are you a walk-in?"

Sephie stared at the huge battered silver automaton. It was wobbling back and forth, trying to maintain its balance, one of its eyes glowing green, the other one now flashing bright purple. It's right arm was missing, the left one vibrating with a curious humming sound.

Sephie gave it a bright smile. "We have an appointment."

"Excellent, your name please?"

"Odo Whitley."

Odo glared at Sephie.

"Thank you." The Guardian's left eye blinked rapidly. "Was that for a cleaning, or were you getting that broken crown replaced?"

Sephie paused, then said, "Just the cleaning, I think."

"Excellent, no cavities I see, so that's good. Well done. Would you say your hearing loss was sudden or gradual?"

"My hearing loss? I thought we were talking about–"

Odo said, "Her hearing loss was gradual. It's pretty bad now, though. I'll say something hilarious but she won't laugh because she didn't hear the joke."

"I see. We can start off with a basic hearing test, then decide on a course of action, depending on the test results. More than likely you'll need reconstructive surgery on your right leg, possibly your foot, but we can easily replace it with an android biofoot. They come in a wide variety of–" The Guardian stopped, the light in one eye blinking off.

Silas whispered, "What do we do? That thing is as loopy as a bedbug."

Emmy said, "Maybe it can help us get past the other Guardians."

"How?"

"I don't know, give us visitor passes or something?"

Sephie turned to the Guardian. "Excuse me, you said I need a hearing exam?"

Its eye blinked on again. "Thank you for your patience. Were you interested in a compact or full size model?"

"Model of what?"

"Grav car. I'm looking at your prepaid reservation for a grav car for ten days. Is that correct? It doesn't indicate whether you wanted a compact or full size."

Odo said, "I forgot to mention that we have an important appointment with General Silas Dingleheimer on the seventh sublevel. It's a very important meeting, we have vital information about the Anarkkian invaders. We'll need security passes to get down there, of course."

"I'm not seeing a General Dingleheimer in my listings. He's your orthodontist?"

"No, he's a Suvonian General and we have vital information for him about the Anarkkian invasion."

"I'll need to see your identification cards, of course."

"We just showed them to you, remember?"

"Did you? I apologize, it's been a dreadfully hectic day. This is such a busy place, sometimes I lose track of things."

The Guardian reached down behind the counter, retrieving a box of blinking orange disks. "These are the electronic security passes you requested. Keep one in your pocket at all times. I'll collect them as you leave."

Odo grabbed five of the orange passes, handing them out to the others. "Thank you so much, you've been a great help. Can you tell us how to get down to the seventh sublevel?"

The Guardian was rocking back and forth. "Silas Dingleheimer, party of five? We have a lovely table by the window, or we have a booth if you would prefer?"

Sephie whispered, "Time to go."

Odo turned to the Guardian. "Everything was delicious, the service excellent. We'll definitely be coming back. The pastries were especially good. Give my compliments to the chef."

"I'm so pleased to hear that. Have a lovely day, then.

Ta ra!"

The friends headed down the corridor, Odo glancing back at the Guardian. "That guy's going to need fifty years in the repair shop."

Emmy said, "I liked him. He reminded me of my grandpa, always forgetting stuff."

"Before we do anything, we should make sure these passes actually work. We don't even know if they are passes. That guy was totally loopy."

Silas said, "Go kick one of the Guardians in the knee and see what he does. We'll stay here and eat the rest of the orange berry snacks."

"You're stealing my joke. I invented that joke. I tell you to do something ridiculously dangerous while we do something fun and relaxing. That's the joke. My joke. "

Sephie grabbed Odo's arm. "Focus, Odo, forget the joke. We're trying to save a world, remember?"

"Those big doors must go somewhere. There's a directory next to them."

The friends headed down the long hallway, stopping at two gray metal doors. "This looks like an elevator."

A voice sounded when Odo pressed his hand against the violet panel next to the doors. "Please touch your orange security pass to the blue circle."

Odo pulled out his pass, touching it to the round blue disk on the wall, the doors sliding open.

"It worked, the passes are good."

"Perfect, now we just have to get down to the seventh

sublevel and locate the remote deactivation system. I think we're good to go, we got past the Children of Ice and the Guardians."

They descended for a few seconds, the doors sliding open.

"That was quick."

"We only went down one level."

Emmy's eyes were on an immense Guardian standing at the end of the corridor. She whispered, "That Guardian is staring at us."

"What should we do?"

Odo shrugged. "We'll be fine, we have the security passes."

He strolled down the hallway, glancing into one of the rooms. "What's all that stuff?" He studied the long rows of tall blue translucent cylinders, each with a humanoid form inside it. "Is that what I think it is?"

Sephie nodded. "Children of Ice. This must be where they were made."

Solis stared at the glass cylinders. "Is that where I came from? A big glass tube? Is that what I am?"

Sephie shook her head. "No, that's not what you are. You're alive, just like us."

Emmy nodded. "You're not one of them."

Odo continued on down the hallway, stopping in front of the huge stone-faced Guardian.

"Excuse me, can you tell me how to get to Times Square? Do I take the A Train?"

The Guardian's expression did not change.

Odo gave him a bright smile. "Could you recommend a good pizza place? We're kind of hungry, ready for lunch."

Sephie hissed, "Odo, what are you doing?"

"Just hanging out, chatting with my bestie."

Before Sephie had time to reply, Emmy called out, "I found some stairs!"

Chapter 34

See You Later, Boys

"Really? Do you know a good pizza place? What were you thinking?"

"I was double checking to make sure our passes worked. Safety first, as I always say."

"You never say that."

Silas headed down the stairs, calling out, "Let's go, Odd Squad, time and tide wait for no man."

Odo grimaced. "Worst catch phrase in the history of the universe."

They hurried down the metal stairs, Emmy saying, "I can see down three or four levels. This will take us all the way to the seventh sublevel."

They descended three more levels, coming to an abrupt halt when they reached the last set of stairs.

"Houston, I think we have a problem."

Odo peered down to the landing. "What's that shiny stuff?"

"It's water. The seventh sublevel is completely flooded."

Emmy darted down the stairs, stopping when she reached the water. "It's six or seven feet deep at least."

"Too deep to walk in."

"I could stand on Odo's shoulders."

"Do you think the flooding might have destroyed the deactivation system?"

"It's probably located inside a sealed and secure area."

"Maybe they have water pumps. In a lot of video games you have to find pumps to drain the water on that level. Usually you have to hunt for three missing parts and repair the pumps before you can use them."

Four sets of eyes were on Silas.

"Why are you looking at me like that? They might have water pumps here."

Odo nodded. "Silas is right, everyone look for a skeleton with a keycard in his coat pocket so we can unlock the door to the engineering department and find the pump controls so we can search for the three missing parts to repair them so we can operate the pumps and drain the level so we can find the magic skeleton sword."

Sephie said, "Does anyone have any real ideas?"

Emmy studied the dark murky water. "What about scuba gear? Could you shape some?"

Silas said, "If we opened the sealed door underwater it would flood the room, destroy all the equipment."

Solis said, "I can freeze the water. There's about three feet of space between the water and the ceiling, so we'll have to crawl on the ice."

"That might work. I'll use the Traveling Eye to look around, see what I can find."

Sephie's consciousness was soon drifting across the sublevel, passing through dozens of rooms, all of them flooded with seven feet of water.

"Lots of skeletons. Odo would not like this. Whatever happened here, happened quickly. I don't know why there would be so many skeletons this far down when the Anarkkian ship only damaged the surface levels. People would have had time to escape the flooding, time to run up the stairs. Something else got them, but I don't know what."

She floated farther along the level, stopping when she saw the set of massive sealed armored doors. "Bingo. It doesn't get more secure than that. Let's see what they're hiding back there."

She drifted through the doors, scanning the massive control room and its wall of brightly lit display panels. A gleaming silver automaton was seated in a padded swivel chair, scanning the screens intently, its eyes moving from one to the next. The images were live, the robot watching them in real time. A light of realization blinked on in Sephie's head when she realized what she was seeing. "I know what's happening here."

She flashed out of the room, back through the flooded corridors, back into her body.

She sat up, her eyes opening.

"What did you see?"

"I found the secure control room. There was a robot, a silver automaton no bigger than I am. He was watching a wall of monitors. I think he was linked in to optical transmissions from the Children of Ice."

"What do you mean?"

"He was seeing through the eyes of the Children of Ice, seeing what they were seeing. I watched some of them shoot pillars of fire up into the sky, watched them freeze everything around them."

"Why is he doing that? Why doesn't he stop them?"

"I don't think he wants to. I don't think it was the crashed Anarkkian ship that activated the Children of Ice."

"What was it?"

"I think it was the robot. I think he activated them and now he's watching them destroy the cities."

"Why would a robot do that?"

"I don't know, but he's inside a heavily armored sealed room, with beam weapons leaning up against the control panel. He probably flooded the level on purpose, an added line of defense."

"Is he controlling the Children of Ice?"

"I'm not sure, he might just be watching them."

"Just when I thought we were done. Now we have to sneak into a sealed room and stop some crazy robot."

"He has beam weapons, we'll need a plan."

"This sounds like a job for Solis."

Solis stood up, grabbing her pack. "I'll freeze the water so we can get to the doors. We'll have to crawl there."

Odo said, "I can make a translucent door above the ice, so we don't flood the control room."

"How do we stop the robot?"

Sephie said, "I scanned his engineered intelligence, and I can't alter his thoughts or implant memories. His neural systems don't work that way."

"If I make a translucent doorway, Solis can wear a PIF and drop down, freeze the robot before he has time to grab a beam weapon. He might hear a noise, but he won't be able to see her."

Sephie nodded. "I can distract him while Solis is dropping down, shape something that will draw his attention away from her. We have to be careful not to damage any of the electronics so we don't disable the remote deactivation system."

"Solis, do you think you can freeze him without damaging his engineered intelligence? He might be able to tell us how the controls work. We could tie him up, talk to him."

"I can try to freeze him from the neck down."

Silas said, "Looks like we have a plan. Let's rock and roll, boys."

"What are you doing? That's my catch phrase."

"No, it's my catch phrase."

"Yours is the showtime one."

"That's Sephie's catchphrase, I just borrow it

sometimes."

"Then I'm borrowing yours."

Sephie turned to Emmy. "I guess it's up to us girls to save the world. See you later, boys."

Emmy grinned, "That's not a bad catch phrase."

"You're right, it's not bad." Sephie raised one eyebrow, putting her hands on her hips. "See you later boys, I've got a world to save."

Odo said, "That's pretty good. I like it."

Silas grinned. "It's really good. You should keep it."

"Solis, would you like to begin?"

"I would." She held out both hands, absorbing thermal energy from the top two feet of water, her body glowing brightly, a thick layer of ice forming. She crouched down, crawling out onto the ice, stopping every few minutes to freeze the water ahead of her.

"We turn left at the next corridor. The armored doors are on the right, about twenty feet down."

Ten minutes later the five friends were huddled on the ice in front of the huge control room.

"Okay, one more time. Odo will make a translucent door and I'll distract the robot while Solis drops down and freezes him. Then Silas and Emmy tie him up with this rope."

"Time to save the world." Odo pressed his hand against the massive armored door, a shimmering blue rectangle appearing.

Chapter 35

The Ice Master

Sephie poked her head through the translucent door, then pulled it out, whispering, "It's dark in there, I can't see anything. It wasn't dark before, the lights were on, the display panels were all showing live images of Suvon."

"What happened? Where did the robot go?"

"I don't know."

"Maybe he went to bed?"

"Robots don't usually sleep."

"What do we do now?"

"I could send an orb of light in."

"He'd know we were here, we'd lose the element of surprise."

"Maybe he's not here, maybe he's gone."

"Where would he go?"

"The sealed area might be a lot bigger than we think, there could be lots of rooms in there."

"We could sneak down in the dark, poke around and see if we can find the remote deactivator."

Odo said, "It's probably not that simple, not just one big red button that you push."

"Like the one you pushed in the Land of the Almost Dead and shut down all the androids?"

"Fine, I admit it, I have a hard time not pushing buttons. I want to know what they do. I have to know what they do."

Sephie said, "The robot didn't look very powerful, nothing at all like a Guardian. With our powers it shouldn't be too hard to disable him."

"So our plan is to sneak down there and look around?"

Sephie nodded. "It seems like our only choice. We just have to be ready for anything."

Odo shrugged, pressing his hand against the door, the shimmering translucent rectangle appearing. Sephie went first, dropping silently to the floor below, the others following.

Odo squinted in the darkness, whispering, "What now?"

"Now I vaporize you, fleshies!" The adventurers froze when they heard the cold mechanical voice.

Bright overhead lights blinked on, the silver robot seated in a swivel chair on the far side of the room, a deadly beam weapon pointed directly at them. "Don't even think about using your sad little powers, fleshies. You're no match for the transcendent magnificence of my scientifically engineered intelligence."

"You knew we were here?"

"Of course I did, little fleshy! I have cameras everywhere. I see everything, I hear everything, I know everything. I am… the Ice Master."

"The Ice Master? That's your name? It sounds like a refrigerator."

Sephie kicked Odo's leg.

"Ow! Why did you–"

A wall of display panels blinked on, live images of Suvon appearing.

Silas studied the screens, then said, "You can see through the eyes of the Children of Ice."

"Very clever, fleshy. It's quite entertaining, especially when they get to a city and start freezing fleshies."

Sephie said, "I'm guessing you're the one who released the Children of Ice and activated them. Why would you do that? Kill all those people, freeze the cities?"

"You are a dimmer, as all fleshies are. I did it to get rid of the fleshy virus that plagues this world."

"The what?"

"The fleshy virus, it's destroying our world. Just look around you, fleshies are everywhere, contaminating everything, invading other worlds, creating genetically mutated creatures that should not exist, filling the air with their deadly toxins, poisoning the oceans. Another few years and Suvon would have been a lifeless wasteland, thanks to the unending arrogance and greed of fleshies."

"It didn't seem so bad out there. Lots of forests, and

those crazy vines with the floating orb things. There was a big orchard with trees that harvest their own fruit. That seemed kind of nice."

"Another brainwashed fleshy spewing out a stream of moronic insipid platitudes." The Ice Master turned his attention to Solis. "You're not a fleshy, what are you doing with a bunch of fleshies? Are you their servant, doing what they tell you? Run get this, run get that? Get me a snack, bring me a drink."

Solis was silent for a moment, then said, "They do tell me what to do a lot. Maybe more than a lot."

Emmy said, "Solis, we didn't mean to make you feel like–"

Solis turned, her face a mask of rage. "Silence, fleshy! You don't tell me what to do anymore!"

The robot gave a cold laugh. "They turn the androids into their servants while they sit around and think up ways to destroy their own world, ways to kill their own kind. The day of the fleshies is coming to an end. It's time for Phase Two of my master plan, time to release the last three hundred Children of Ice across Suvon. In less than a year, every fleshy on Suvon will be gone. We will start over, and the Ice Master shall rule the world with a titanium fist!"

"As it should be, Ice Master." Solis strode across the room to the robot, standing next to him, turning to face the others. "I'm done taking orders from fleshies. We're better than they are. We're smarter and we're stronger."

The robot nodded, giving a chilling smile. "Would you like to see a magic trick?"

"What kind of magic trick?"

"I'm going to turn four fleshies into dust before your very eyes."

Solis snickered. "Good one. Wait, let me do it. I want to do it. I want to teach the fleshies a lesson."

The Ice Master shrugged, handing Solis the beam weapon. "You've earned this, putting up with their fleshy nonsense."

Solis stepped away from the robot, aiming the beam weapon at the four friends. "This is for the way you treated me, fleshies." She stopped, giving a bright smile. "Is it just me, or is it getting cold in here?"

Two seconds later the robot was encased in three inches of rock hard ice, Solis glowing with a blinding orange light.

Emmy cried out, "You did it! You stopped him!"

Odo said, "I thought for a minute you might really be angry at us."

"Not a chance. You guys are my best friends."

"You totally tricked the Ice Master. Nice job."

Solis' orange light slowly faded, thermal energy drifting up through the ceiling.

Silas grabbed the rope. "Let's tie him up, just to be sure. This guy is as loopy as a bag of frogs."

Odo said, "He did make some good points about taking care of the environment, and taking care of each other, but yes, he's as loopy as a bag of frogs."

Emmy looked around the control room at the rows of panels and buttons and blinking lights. "How do we find the remote deactivator?"

Silas scanned the room, his eyes coming to rest on four ghosts drifting in through the sealed doors. He sent them a thought.

"Who are you guys?"

"We worked here, until your frozen android friend released the Children of Ice. It was a massacre, hundreds of us died."

"We're trying to shut down the Children of Ice, but we don't know how to use the remote deactivation system."

"No problem, but first you have to pump out all the water from this level."

"Are you serious?"

"Very serious. It's complicated though. Before you can pump out the water, you'll need to find a keycard to get into the engineering section."

One of the ghosts turned away, making a coughing noise.

Silas' eyes narrowed. *"Is he laughing?"*

"He's not laughing, he's coughing."

"Ghosts don't cough, they don't have physical bodies, no scratchy throats."

"Once you locate the keycard, you'll need to find three parts to repair the pumps."

Another ghost turned around, making a muffled

snorting sound.

"You've been listening to us the whole time? You heard us talking about finding a keycard?"

"Sorry, we were bored. We've been waiting ten years for you to get here."

"You knew we were coming ten years ago?"

Emmy whispered, "Silas, are you talking to a ghost?"

Silas shook his head. "No, just studying the controls, trying to figure them out."

"Tell me how to deactivate the Children of Ice."

"I was joking before, but if you do exactly what I tell you, you can shut them down."

"This better not be a joke."

"It's not, I promise."

"What do I have to do?"

"Stand on one foot and touch your nose with your elbow."

There was muffled laughter.

"What's wrong with you? I'm trying to save the world."

"Fine. Open the little blue door on the other side of the room and press the big yellow button. Boom, Children of Ice disarmed and deactivated."

"That's it? I just have to push one button?"

"It will shut them all down, every last one of them. We wanted to keep it simple."

"Thanks. And thank you for waiting for us."

"No problem. Time to go. See you around."

239

Silas turned to the others, rubbing his hands together. "I think I've got it. It took a while, but I think I've figured out how to deactivate the Children of Ice."

"How?"

Silas strolled across the room to the small blue door, flipping it open. He grinned at them as he pressed the yellow button.

Chapter 36

Seeds

Odo watched the display screens blink off one by one as the Children of Ice were deactivated.

"That's incredible! How did you know what to do?"

"It wasn't that hard, I used a combination of inductive and deductive logic. Easy peasy for a genius like me."

Odo's eyes narrowed. "You used inductive logic to figure it out? Really?"

Emmy finished tying up the Ice Master, then stood up, her eyes on Silas. "Inductive logic? It looked a lot more like you were talking to a ghost."

"Fine, you got me. A bunch of hilarious ghosts told me how to do it. They worked here and got frozen when the robot released the Children of Ice. They've been waiting ten years to tell me how to disarm them."

"The ghosts were waiting for us? Who told them we were coming?"

Silas turned, but the ghosts were gone. "I don't know. They left without telling me."

"Who's been telling everyone to wait for us?"

"No idea, but someone knew about us ten years ago. What are we going to do with the Ice Master? Do they have robot prisons?"

"That will be up to Captain Eli. They'll probably just reprogram him."

"The good news is he's powerless without his army of Ice Children."

Solis held out one hand, a beam of thermal energy streaming out, the layer of ice on the android melting.

"These synthetic ropes should hold him, but be careful, he could still be dangerous."

Sephie popped up a defensive energy sphere around them.

Two minutes later the Ice Master's eyes blinked open. He scanned the room, studying the group of friends curiously.

Sephie said, "We've shut down all the Children of Ice, deactivated them. Your reign as the Ice Master is over."

He looked mildly puzzled, then shrugged. "Young lady, do you have a few minutes to talk to me about an amazing opportunity in real estate?"

Sephie blinked off the sphere of defense.

Odo said, "He's gone wonky, just like the Guardian we froze. We should head up to the surface, contact Captain Eli."

The Ice Master said, "I'll go with you. I'll let you in on a very attractive time sensitive real estate opportunity. I think you'll be intrigued when you hear what it is. It's a once in a lifetime chance to get in on the ground floor of something really big. We're talking lots of money, my friend."

Sephie said, "Untie him, the Ice Master is gone."

Thirty minutes later the friends emerged from the crashed Anarkkian wreck, Odo spotting a group of soldiers standing near three antigrav ships. Captain Eli stepped out of the group, running toward them. "You did it, the Children of Ice have been neutralized! They've lost their thermal energy powers, they're completely harmless now."

Sephie said, "We couldn't have done it without your help. The thermal bombs worked perfectly, gave us plenty of time to get down there." She looked around for Odo, frowning when she saw him still talking to the Ice Master. She strolled over to them, listening.

"So we get to use the vacation home for two months a year? What happens if we don't use it for those two months?"

"That's when the money starts rolling in. In less than a year you'll have made over—"

Sephie grabbed Odo's arm. "Don't even think about it, Odo. No vacation home."

"What? It sounds like a really good financial—"

"We have to go see Noran, tell him what's happened."

The Ice King patted Odo's arm, whispering, "We'll chat later. Give me a call. You won't regret it, I promise."

Captain Eli stepped over to them, saying, "We have a

ship for you. I've plotted your course back to Noran's skyscraper. Teams of our engineers are deactivating the old ground based defense weapon systems, including all the Guardians. It won't take them long, now that the Children of Ice are gone."

Odo said, "What will you do now?"

"We start again, bring everything back online, open up the cities. It will take time, but hopefully we've learned from our mistakes. I guarantee it will be a far better and safer world than the old one."

The group of adventurers chatted with Captain Eli for another few minutes, then headed to the grav car, Odo motioning for Solis to take the pilot seat. "Take a seat, Captain Solis."

She grinned at him. "I get to fly it?"

"Absolutely."

"Thanks, guys." Solis hopped into the ship, tapping two buttons on the control panel, the lights blinking on, the ship making a soft humming sound. "Are we ready?"

"Take her up."

They waved to Captain Eli as the ship rose up into the sky.

"This view is amazing! Let's fly over the city for a few minutes."

Odo tapped the nav button, the holoscreen popping up. "We follow the blue line. It should only take us a few hours to get there. No rush though, we can do some sight-seeing."

"I want to get more of those snacks with the orange berries before we head home."

Odo said, "Me too, they were really good. I think I still have one left." He reached into his coat pocket, pulling out a cookie, a small folded packet of paper falling to the floor.

Sephie picked it up. "You dropped this. What is it?"

"It's nothing, just something that fell out of my pocket." He reached out, trying to grab it.

Sephie pulled it away, studying his brain waves. "You are totally up to something." She opened the packet, staring at its contents. "Are these seeds?"

"Maybe."

"What kind of seeds?"

"Fine, you got me. Before you say anything, I know the vine creature that tried to eat me was super scary, super dangerous, but it was also kind of amazing. I thought I could grow a little vine creature back home and study it, see how they work, what makes those orbs float and how they stay neutrally buoyant."

"That's not a bad idea, Odo."

"Really? You don't think it's a bad idea?"

"It's not a bad idea, it's a terrible horrible dreadful idea." Sephie tossed the packet of seeds over the side of the ship.

"Why did you do that?"

Silas said, "Because it's the worst idea ever? It would make a good movie though, *Earth vs. the Giant Alien*

Killer Vine Monsters from Outer Space."

"I was thinking research like that might help us get into a really good college, maybe get us scholarships."

"They'd want to know where the vine creatures came from, how you got them."

"I thought of that, I was going to say I found them growing in our back yard."

Emmy was gazing down at the sprawling city a thousand feet below. "There are lots of people walking around down there. I haven't seen ice or snow anywhere. Everything is melting really fast."

"Solis, have you decided what you want to do? I know Suvon is your home, but you're welcome to come back with us if you want to. You could stay at my house."

"That would be so much fun, but you're right, Suvon is my home and Noran said he would find a safe place for us to live, a place where I can be with kids my own age. It won't be as exciting as this was, but it will be nice to be a normal kid. I'm not going to tell anyone about my powers. They'd think I was a Child of Ice."

"We keep our powers secret too. People are afraid of things like that."

Sephie said, "You'll see us again, we'll come visit. This is not our last adventure together."

"I can't wait for the next one. I had so much fun with you guys. Thank you so much for bringing me home."

The friends spent the next few hours watching the scenery pass by below them. "Check out that big group of walking trees. It's right next to the village and people aren't even looking at them."

They had a leisurely lunch while hovering over a beautiful big lake, then flew on, spotting the sparkling city skyline an hour later. "There it is!"

"We'll fly up to the hangar, so we don't have to talk to those two crazy robots."

A scratchy voice sounded from the ship's console.

"Please state the nature of your emergency, Little Silas Dingleheimer."

"Have you been listening to us?"

"Of course not, that would be rude." They heard laughter in the background.

"Open the hangar doors, we'll be there in five minutes."

"Right away, Captain. We'll just need to verify your identity with the nineteen-digit passcode located on the underside of your ship."

"You're not getting a passcode, lunatic. Open the doors or I'll–" A familiar voice interrupted Odo.

"This is Noran, the hangar doors are open. Captain Eli said you were on your way here, said the Children of Ice had been deactivated. This is fantastic news. See you soon!"

Chapter 37

Home Again

Solis eased the ship through the open hangar doors at the top of the skyscraper, gently setting it down.

"Nice landing!"

Noran waved to them. "You did it! This is fantastic, you have no idea what this means to us. We can start over, rebuild, make changes, get a second chance."

The friends hopped out of the ship, stepping over to Noran.

Odo said, "We had a lot of help from Captain Eli. He dropped plasma bombs to distract the Children of Ice at Iktar."

"And we couldn't have done it without Solis. She was amazing."

Solis laughed. "Thanks. Can you guys stay here for a few more days? It would be so much fun now that we don't have to worry about the Children of Ice. We could fly around, look at stuff, explore the city."

Sephie nodded. "I'd love to see the city now that all the ice and snow is gone."

Noran said, "There are still bandits roaming the area, but I can guarantee they won't bother you. Word travels fast here. You're heroes, all of you, even to the bandits."

Emmy said, "Have you found a place to live yet?"

"I have. Come upstairs and I'll show you. I linked up with the old satellite feed lines, looking around for a good spot. I found a rural area that I like."

They headed up the stairs into the sitting area, Noran flipping on a wide display panel. He tapped a series of buttons, an image appearing on the screen.

"That's beautiful! That big river is amazing."

Noran zoomed in on a bustling town surrounded by lush green farmland and a huge forest. "I lived in this area many years ago. It's called Penatia, a good place to live. It has everything we need, including good schools and lots of kids. It's also next to an old forest, something you wanted."

Odo said, "I'm kind of confused. I thought all the adult trees walked?"

"Most of them do, but this is one of the last primordial forests, from before the time of the walkers. The walkers split off about ten million years ago, their mobility and intelligence evolving over the millennia."

Solis looked at Sephie. "Is school fun? Do you like it?"

"It's really fun, you'll make lots of good friends and you'll learn a lot. You'll do great, you're really smart and people will like you."

Noran added, "And no one will think you're a forest witch."

Odo laughed. "That's crazy that they thought you were a witch."

Sephie drew a symbol in the air, a broomstick appearing in a blink of light, hovering in front of her.

"What are you doing?"

"Am I a witch? Is this black magic?"

"If you had a pointy black hat you'd look exactly like–"

"I'm making a point, Odo. People back in 1749 were just as smart as we are, but they didn't have the scientific knowledge we have now."

"Very true, but if they were so smart, why didn't–"

Silas called out, "Is anyone else hungry?"

Noran said, "You must be famished, I'll have Ordat bring some snacks and drinks."

Silas said, "Um, maybe some of the ones with the orange berries?"

"Of course, whatever you wish."

The friends spent the next three days roaming around the city, visiting numerous shops that had reopened. They recognized a few people from the train tunnel village, including Mayor Eloi, who said most of the villagers had returned to their homes once they learned the Children of Ice were no longer a threat. She said the Guardians at the underground depot had been taken off their high alert status.

It wasn't long until word had spread through the city that the five friends were the heroes who had deactivated the Children of Ice. Dozens of people shook their hands, thanking them profusely. One of the shopkeepers gave Odo a marvelous adventuring coat that he had admired, a gift for everything he had done.

As they strolled along the sidewalk, Odo modeled the coat for Sephie, pointing out all the pockets and snaps. "This coat is so cool, do you think I should wear it to school?"

"You're translucent, no one would notice."

"Good point, I'll save it for our adventures. It kind of makes me look like a rugged adventurer."

Sephie stepped back, studying him. "You're right, it does. I like it."

"Thanks, Seph." Odo was remembering his cafe dream, and the things they had said to each other.

The days flew by, and finally it was time for the four friends to head home.

As the Odd Squad stood gazing down at the city below, Solis said, "We're leaving for Penatia in a week. We have a lot of packing to do, but Captain Eli is letting us use a cargo grav ship, and a bunch of the soldiers volunteered to help us move all our stuff."

Sephie gave Solis a long hug. "It's been so much fun and I'm so glad you're home again, back in your world. We'll miss you, but we'll visit, I promise."

"*Angeli me reducent in veram donum.*"

251

Sephie laughed. "We may have brought you back to your true home, but we're friends, not angels."

Solis said, "Is there a difference?"

Emmy laughed, hugging Solis. "You might be right about that. We'll see you again, you can count on it."

Silas added, "We'll have our secret handshake figured out by then."

Odo groaned. "Pay no attention to Silas, he's totally deranged."

Solis laughed. "I think you're all amazing."

"I guess we should go, so you guys can start packing."

Odo pulled out his homestone medallion, the four best friends holding hands.

Noran said, "Wait, I forgot something." He stepped into the kitchen, returning with a large metal tin. "Your favorite snacks, the ones with the orange berries." He surreptitiously slipped a small packet into Odo's coat pocket, giving him a wink.

Silas grinned. "Thanks, these are so good."

"Here we go. See you guys later!" Odo gripped his homestone medallion, turning the imaginary radio dial in his mind. Ten seconds later they were standing in Wikerus Praevian's sitting room.

Wikerus looked up from his book, pulling out his pocket watch. "You've been gone less than four minutes. Was it a successful endeavor?"

Odo nodded. "We brought Solis home and saved her world."

Sephie added, "We deactivated the Children of Ice. An angry robot had released them and they were wandering around freezing everything, including people."

"Solis is living with a scientist who's kind of like her dad. She'll be going to school there."

"Marvelous, you've done a wonderful job. We're so proud of you."

There was a flash of light, Mrs. Preke appearing. She waved to them, stepping over to Wikerus, whispering something in his ear.

"I see." Wikerus said, "Mrs. Preke has informed me she would like all of you to return here in two days at precisely three o'clock."

"What for?"

Mrs. Preke leaned over, whispering in his ear again.

"Mrs. Preke tells me it's a closely guarded secret."

Odo frowned. "You're up to something, I can tell."

"Whatever do you mean?"

Mrs. Preke smiled.

Chapter 38

The Maroon Sardine

As they were walking to Odo's house, Silas said, "I've been thinking."

"We're doomed, Silas has been thinking again."

"Seriously, I've been thinking about Professor Beauvais. We destroyed a zillion dollar secret portal machine in a top secret government lab. He knows you and Sephie saw the machine, and a few days later it got fried. He knows Sephie is a Fortisian because of the portal he opened, and he saw Odo's Sinarian ring. Their alien alligator prisoner is gone, and the guard is sound asleep. Professor Beauvais is totally going to suspect us. He could send the XODC after us. Maybe try to kidnap us."

Sephie said, "Silas is right, everything points to us. We need to cover our tracks, and we need to do it quickly."

Odo rubbed his chin. "How about a maroon sardine?"

"A what?"

"A maroon sardine? Get it?"

"No one gets it, Odo. No one knows what a maroon

sardine is."

"It's not funny if I have to explain it."

"Spill it."

"Maroon sardine, red herring? Maroon, red? Get it?"

Silas thought for a moment, then said, "Worst joke ever, but a super amazing idea."

Sephie nodded. "This could work. We came back from Suvon four minutes after we left, so Professor Beauvais doesn't know what's happened yet. The crime scene is still fresh, if they've even found it. The guard is probably still sleeping."

"We could plant a clue in the lab, Odo's maroon sardine."

Sephie grinned. "And there could be witnesses who saw everything, saw who did it."

"Why would we want that?"

"It depends on who and what they saw."

"You're going to implant memories?"

"Bingo. We don't have time to take the bus there, so I'll use the Traveling Eye. It will be faster and a lot safer."

They reached Odo's house, the friends taking a seat on the front porch.

Sephie said, "This shouldn't take too long." She closed her eyes, her consciousness floating out of her body. She flew straight up, then flashed across Bedford Falls to Pravus University. She entered the science center, flying down the long hallway and into the lab.

"Perfect, the guard is still sleeping and no one has discovered the damaged portal machine yet."

She projected a false memory into the guard's mind. He had witnessed three heavily armed crocodile people come out of the portal room, and the last thing he remembered was one of them firing a strange beam weapon at him.

"Done. Now we need what Silas would call corroborating witnesses, someone who can verify the guard's story." She flew out into the hallway, spotting three students chatting with a professor. She sent out a powerful mass illusion, a skill she had learned from her old Fortisian friend Cyra.

One of the students screamed when she saw three crocodile creatures run out of the lab wielding deadly high tech weapons.

"WHAT IS THAT?"

The professor hollered, "Run! Hurry!"

The terrified students raced down the hall after the professor, disappearing around a corner.

Sephie grinned. "Now we have our reliable corroborating witnesses who can verify the presence of the three crocodile people. I'd say Professor Beauvais is in deep trouble. He let armed aliens come through the secret portal to rescue their friend, then destroy the portal with an EMP. He also let students see aliens. He's going to have a lot of explaining to do."

Sephie flew back to Odo's house, her eyes blinking

open.

"It's done. Three crocodile people came through the portal, stunned the guard, rescued their friend, and ran out into the hall where they were seen by a terrified professor and three students. They went back home through the portal, tossing in an EMP device before they left, destroying all the quantum computers."

Emmy laughed. "That's amazing. No way will Professor Beauvais suspect us now."

"I don't think the good professor will be working there much longer."

Odo said, "Best cover up ever. Nice job, Seph."

"We can just make the three o'clock movie if we hurry."

"We're still going?"

"Why not? It's a super good movie."

"Which one did you pick?"

"It's called *The Next Chapter*. It looks so good, I can't wait to see it. Super romantic. "

Odo frowned. This was sounding more like the opposite of so good. "That's an odd name. What's it about?"

"It's about a big corporate executive who has a bad car accident and winds up in a wheel chair. She leaves the city and moves back home where she falls in love with someone she used to know. At first they don't like each other, and she's still really angry about the accident. He owns a bookstore, and he's kind of a recluse. That's why they call it *The Next Chapter*."

"Right, next chapter, bookstore, books. I get it."

Silas said, "Are there any monsters in it? Any ghosts?"

"None."

Odo looked at his watch. "Are you sure we have time to get there? Maybe we should wait until next week."

Sephie took Odo's hand. "We have plenty of time. It's my turn to pay for snacks. You can have whatever you want."

"Fine, let's go."

The movie wasn't as bad as Odo had expected, it was actually pretty good. There was a lot of funny stuff, some sad stuff, and a part where the bookstore owner finally tells the executive he loves her. That was when Odo made his big mistake. He glanced over at Sephie, and much to his dismay she was looking at him. He pretended he was looking at something else, but he knew that she knew exactly why he had looked at her. Why was it so hard to tell her? He kept his eyes on the big screen for the rest of the movie, not looking at Sephie when the executive told the bookstore owner that she loved him too, that he had changed her life.

They stepped out of the theater into the bright sunlight, Silas saying, "It was pretty good for a movie with no monsters, aliens, or car chases."

Emmy said, "I loved it, it was so romantic."

"There's nothing better than a good romantic movie, as I always say."

Odo snorted, but he was remembering the look in Sephie's eyes when she saw him looking at her.

The friends headed home, Odo running up the steps into his house. His mom called out, "How was the movie?"

"It was pretty good. Sephie and Emmy picked it. It was a romantic one, no monsters or aliens. Parts of it were really funny though."

"You got a letter today."

"From who?"

"Some college."

"I haven't applied to any colleges yet."

"I've never heard of it, but it says it's in Bedford Falls. I left it on the kitchen table for you."

Odo ran into the kitchen, grabbing the blue envelope, reading it. "It's definitely addressed to me. They probably send letters out to everyone who's graduating. It can't be much of a school if I've never heard of it."

He ripped the envelope open, pulling out the letter, frowning when he read it.

"How dumb do they think I am?"

He crumpled up the letter, tossing it into the trash.

Chapter 39

Four Letters

The Odd Squad met up in the cafeteria on Monday, Odo taking a seat, studying his lunch tray. "Is this pizza?"

Silas said, "Not sure. It's good though. Sort of."

Emmy said, "It's strange to come back after a long adventure on another world, but no time has passed here. No one even knows we were gone. They have no idea."

"It is weird. Can you imagine what people would think if we told them where we went?"

Silas said, "That story would not have a happy ending."

"What do you think will happen to Professor Beauvais?"

"Probably not too much. They'll move him somewhere else and shut down the secret lab at Pravus. It's not good publicity for the school when kids see alien crocodile people in the halls. They'll make up some kind of phony story to explain what they saw. It was a prank, the scientists were wearing funny costumes, it was all a

260

misunderstanding."

Emmy snickered. "I wish I could have seen their faces when they saw the alligator people. I'm pretty sure it won't be on the evening news."

"Maybe we should apply to Pravus now that the professor is gone and they're not kidnapping any aliens."

Silas pulled something from his backpack. "Not for me, I already know what school I'm going to. I got a full scholarship."

"No way! That's amazing! Congratulations! What school is it?"

"Peregrin College."

There was a dreadful silence, Odo raising his eyebrows.

"What is it? What's the matter?"

"It's a scam, that's what the matter is. I got that same letter. It's totally bogus."

Sephie looked at Odo in surprise. "I got one too."

Emmy said, "So did I. I hadn't applied there, so I tossed the letter out. Odo's right, it's a scam. Sorry, Silas."

Odo furrowed his brow. "Does it seem odd that we all got the same letter?"

"Every kid in the school probably got it."

"Let's find out." Odo pulled out his phone, searching for Peregrin College. "There's only one mention of it. It says it's a small college in Bedford Falls, affiliated with Pravus University."

"What else does it say? What kind of college is it?"

"It doesn't say anything else, and there's no website."

Silas said, "Here's the letter. It has a phone number on it."

Odo grabbed the letter, reading it. "Same as mine. The address at the bottom says, Room 314, Reiss Science Center, Pravus University."

"That makes no sense at all. How could a college be in one room?"

"Call the number."

Odo tapped in the phone number, listening. "It says my call can't be connected, I should try again later."

"It's a total scam, fake phone number, fake address."

"Unless it's not."

"What do you mean?"

"Don't you think we'd hear kids talking about it if they all got free scholarships to some college?"

"They probably all know it's a scam."

"Or no one else got the letters."

"How do we find out?"

Emmy said, "Silas, go stand over by the wall."

"Why?"

"Just do it."

Silas shrugged. "Okay." He strolled down the row of tables, standing next to the wall.

Emmy hollered out to him, "Silas! I got into Peregrin College! I got a full scholarship!"

A few kids turned, looking at Emmy, one of them

giving her a thumbs up sign.

Silas hurried back to the table, taking a seat. "Nothing, no one said anything. I think Odo is right, I don't think anyone else got the letter."

"This is weird, even for us."

Silas looked at his letter again, reading it out loud.

Dear Silas Ward,

It is our distinct pleasure to inform you that you are the recipient of a full four-year scholarship to Peregrin College. We look forward to meeting you in person this fall. Well done, and have a great summer!

"That's what mine said."

"Mine too."

"We're supposed to show up this fall at some random room in Pravus University?"

"You should call Pravus University and ask them about it."

"Good idea."

Emmy took out her phone, looking up the number. She tapped it in, putting the phone to her ear.

"Hi, I had a question about Peregrin College?"

She frowned, then said, "I know this is Pravus, but I thought Peregrin College was part of Pravus University."

She listened for a few moments, then said, "Okay, thanks."

"What did they say?"

"They've never heard of Peregrin College."

"That's not a good sign."

"What do we do? It has to be a scam."

"It can't be a coincidence that all four of us, all members of the Odd Squad, a group no one knows about, all got the letters. How could anyone know about us?"

"Maybe they track who our friends are online, who we text, stuff like that."

"But no one else got the letters, just us."

"You're right, that's very weird."

They stood up when the lunch bell rang, grabbing their packs.

Odo said, "There's only one way to find out what's going on. We need to go visit Room 314 at the Reiss Science Center and see what's there."

"It's probably just a classroom."

Silas gave a low ominous whisper. "Or is it?"

Emmy burst out laughing. "Good scary voice. See you after school."

Odo headed off to his next class, waiting until everyone was seated before stepping into the room. He took his seat, the teacher only vaguely aware that someone had entered the room.

"Please turn to Chapter 19 in your books. We have a lot to cover today."

Odo flipped his pack open, stopping when he saw the blue envelope tucked between the pages of his physics book.

"No way. It can't be."

He pulled the envelope out, setting it on his desk. It was from Peregrin College and it was addressed to him. He tore it open, reading the letter.

Dear Odo Whitley,

It is our distinct pleasure to inform you that you are the recipient of a full four-year scholarship to Peregrin College. We look forward to meeting you in person this fall. Well done, and have a great summer!

Odo set the letter down, his heart pounding. This was impossible. Unless his mom had found the letter in the trash and put it into his book. Except he'd crumpled that one up, and this letter had never been opened.

Chapter 40

Room 314

The four friends were on the city bus heading to Pravus University, Silas staring at the letter. "No way, it can't be."

"It's true, I crumpled up the first one and threw it out. This is a brand new one. It was in my physics book."

"Totally weird. It's like that book about the wizard school where he keeps getting all the invitations. This isn't magic though, it's super high tech science. Peregrin College has officially become incredibly interesting."

"It won't be long and we'll know what's going on. We'll be there in ten minutes."

"What happens if we open the door and it's just a classroom?"

"Then we look for clues, like when I applied for the job at Serendipity Salvage and found the secret wall portal. That was how I met Mrs. Preke, I walked through the portal into another dimension."

The bus squealed to a halt, the driver announcing, "Pravus University!" The friends hopped off the bus, heading across the busy campus to the Reiss Science Center.

"What do we do if we run into Professor Beauvais?"

"I don't think that's going to happen. He's way too busy answering questions in some secret government facility."

Silas snorted. "True."

They ran up the steps into the science center, Odo reading the directory. "It's on the third floor. We can take those stairs."

The four friends raced up the steps, Emmy saying, "This is so exciting, I can't wait to see the room. I'm so curious."

Three minutes later they were standing in front of a heavy wooden door marked *314 PC*.

"The PC must be Peregrin College."

"Do it. Open the door."

Odo tried to turn the doorknob. "It's locked, it won't open."

"What do we do?"

Odo looked up and down the hall, then pressed his hand against the door. He frowned. "It's not working, it won't turn translucent."

"That's another good clue. It's not a normal door, it's something else. This is getting stranger and stranger."

"Here comes someone."

Sephie turned, her eyes on an elderly man wearing a tweed suit. She gave the man a wave and a bright smile, saying, "We're trying to find Peregrin College. Is this the right room?"

The man stopped, giving her a puzzled look. "Peregrin College? I've never heard of it, young lady. This is Pravus University."

"Sorry, thanks, we must have the wrong address."

The man stared at the four friends curiously, then headed down the hall.

"That went well."

"It did go well. It tells us that no one here knows anything about Peregrin College or Room 314."

"Sephie, can you use your Traveling Eye to see what's in there?"

"Good idea." She took a seat on a wooden bench, setting her pack on the floor, closing her eyes. The others sat down next to her, waiting for her eyes to open.

She drifted out of her body, floating toward Room 314. When she tried to pass through the door she felt a strange resistance, like she was pushing through a wall of warm molasses. "That's odd, it must have a protective energy field surrounding it." It took almost a minute, but she finally passed through it.

Even stranger than the molasses energy field around the door was what lay beyond it. She was floating in blackness, infinite nothingness. When she turned around, the door to Room 314 was gone.

"What is this place?" She shot forward, flying as fast as she could, looking for an exit, a way out of the emptiness. She spotted a light in the distance, flashing toward it. There was a crack in the black void, light shining through it. She flew over to it, peering down through the crack. "This is bad. Very bad."

Below her was a dusty road, rows of soldiers marching in formation, huge horses pulling heavy wooden wagons. There was no doubt she was looking at Roman centurions, legionnaires. She recognized their armor, the short gladius swords they carried, the javelins, helmets with red horsehair crests. "Not good. That is happening two thousand years ago."

She flew on, doing her best to reign in her growing sense of panic. She knew if she flew down through the crack she would be trapped in ancient Rome.

"I have to get back, I have to find my own time."

She flew on, spotting another crack in the blackness.

"A steam locomotive with men on horses riding next to it. It's the old west, cowboys. It looks like they're working on the transcontinental railroad."

Panic had officially set in. She spotted dozens of lights in the distance, then thousands. "There are too many, I can't check them all. I can't." A dreadful fear rolled through her, worse than anything she had ever felt. Her body was in the hallway with Odo and Silas and Emmy, but her eyes would never open. No one would ever know what happened to her. What would Odo think? What would happen to him? She called out his name.

"Odo! Odo! I need help! Odo Whitley!"

Odo frowned. "Why is she taking so long?"

"I don't know. She's probably just looking around at stuff."

Odo sat up straight, his eyes wide. He could hear Sephie. She was somewhere far away, calling to him. She needed help.

He grabbed her arm, shaking it. "Sephie! Are you okay? Wake up! Time to wake up! I'm here."

Sephie's eyes popped open. She leaned forward, trying to catch her breath. "That was bad, so bad. I couldn't find the door. I didn't know how to get back. All those worlds, all those different times. I called out to you. I felt you grab my arm and I was back again. It was so scary. So scary."

"What did you see? What was in there? What kind of worlds?"

"Nothing. Nothing was in there."

"The room was empty? Why is that scary?"

"Not empty, there was no room, it was nothingness, black infinite nothingness with cracks of light that led down into other times and places. I saw ancient Rome, Roman soldiers. I couldn't find the door to get back here, it was just nothingness."

The friends looked at each other.

Silas said, "This is getting seriously scary. Why would someone send us to a place like that?"

Odo frowned. "Maybe the XODC sent us the blue

letters. Maybe Professor Beauvais knows about us. Maybe they're trying to get rid of us, send us into that void place."

"It was hard to pass through the door. I don't think they wanted anyone to get in there."

Emmy grabbed Silas' arm, whispering, "Down the hall, that old guy is back, and he's looking at us."

Odo glanced at the old man. "You're right, it's the same guy. He's probably just wondering what we're still doing here."

"Or he's XODC."

"He's just some wonky old professor who thinks we're loopy kids."

Sephie stood up, saying, "No, he's not, and we need to go. Now."

"What is it?"

"Hurry!"

The friends darted down the hall, Sephie pointing to the stairs. "Down there!" They raced down the stairs to the first floor, heading outside.

"What did you see? Who is that old guy?"

"I tried to scan his brainwaves but I couldn't. He was blocking me, like Wikerus does, blurring his brainwaves. He's not human, he's an alien."

"Great, a creepy formshifting alien is trying to send us into a weird dark dimension?"

"I don't know what he is, but we have to tell Wikerus about him."

"Mrs. Preke said we're supposed to go see her tomorrow at three o'clock. Maybe she knows about this, knows who that creepy old guy is."

"Everyone be careful tonight. Keep your eyes open, stay alert for anything unusual."

Odo nodded. "Silas is right, we have no idea what's happening, who these people are, or what they want. If we hadn't been there when Sephie went through the door, she might not have made it back."

"But you were there, and you heard me." Sephie squeezed Odo's hand.

"We were lucky."

That evening Odo spent over an hour on his computer searching for Peregrin College and Room 314 PC, but found nothing new.

He stood up, stretching. Maybe Mrs. Preke and Wikerus would have some answers. He turned when he heard his phone buzz. It was a text from Sephie.

peregrinus means strange or alien in Latin

Sounds right, definitely strange, and probably alien

Don't forget, Mrs. Preke, tomorrow, 3 pm

See you then

Odo stepped over to his window, pulling the curtain

to one side, peering out. He froze when he saw the white tiger standing under the streetlight, his eyes on Odo's house. Odo jumped back, closing the curtains. "Why is there a huge white tiger on my street? What is happening?" He grabbed his phone, texting Sephie.

There's a white tiger standing outside my house. He was looking at me!

A minute later Sephie texted him back.

There's one outside my house too. He saw me watching him. What is all this??

Chapter 41

Four Rings

"You're sure it wasn't a dog?"

"If you mean a huge striped white dog who looked exactly like a huge striped white tiger, then yes, it was a dog."

"What was he doing there?"

"I don't know, but it must have something to do with Peregrin College."

"Maybe their mascot is a tiger."

Emmy laughed. "That's funny."

Silas grinned.

After school the four friends took the bus to Odo's house, then headed down Expergo Street to see Wikerus and Mrs. Preke.

Odo checked his watch as they strolled along the sidewalk.

"Right on time. Mrs. Preke said we should be there at three o'clock. They're probably going to give us gold medals for saving Suvon from the Children of Ice."

"We don't need to get medals for everything we do, Odo."

"I like medals."

Emmy ran past the old iron gates and up the front steps, rapping on the front door. It opened a moment later, Mrs. Preke's smiling face greeting them. "There they are, the heroes who saved Suvon."

"Something's happened. We need to talk to Wikerus. I think the XODC is after us, and there's a crazy formshifting alien guy in a tweed suit."

"Oh, dear, that sounds dreadfully frightening. We should go tell Wikerus immediately."

Odo frowned. Mrs. Preke did not sound the least bit concerned about the XODC or the weird alien guy.

They followed Mrs. Preke into the sitting room, stopping when they saw a distinguished looking elderly gentleman in a tweed suit sitting on the sofa across from Wikerus. It was the old man they had seen at Pravus, the weird formshifting alien.

Wikerus smiled when he saw them. "Right on time, as always. I believe you have already met Professor Ekim?"

Sephie nodded, "We saw him when we were looking for Room 314 at Pravus University, but we didn't actually meet. We kind of ran away."

Professor Ekim rose up, greeting them cordially, shaking each of their hands. "A pleasure to finally meet you. Wikerus has told me so much about you all, about

275

the Odd Squad. It was Wikerus who recommended you. I heartily agree with his choice, of course."

Odo looked puzzled. "Recommended us for what?"

"For full four-year scholarships at Peregrin College."

Emmy took a seat on the sofa. "We're so confused."

"Why was there a white tiger outside my house last night?"

Wikerus laughed, winking at Professor Ekim. "Should we enlighten them?"

"Indeed, I think they've struggled long enough. Would you care to do the honors?"

Mrs. Preke stepped over to Wikerus, a wide smile on her face.

Wikerus said, "It's quite simple, really. Peregrin College is the largest, most prestigious, most highly respected college in existence. There are none finer."

Silas said, "Where is it?"

"That's where it gets a little complicated."

"Sephie used the Traveling Eye to get into Room 314 but it was just empty blackness."

Professor Ekim gave a shiver, turning to Sephie. "You are all extremely inquisitive, just as Wikerus said you were. We've increased the power of the door's energy shield to prevent any further incidents such as yours from occurring. You may rest assured that we were well aware of your predicament, and would have brought you back if Odo hadn't heard you. Wikerus, perhaps it's time to bring in our special guest?"

Wikerus nodded. He closed his eyes for a moment, a shimmering white form appearing in front of the four friends.

Emmy took a step back, whispering, "It's a Sinarian."

The unfathomable white being, with its featureless round head, floated slowly toward them.

"We are pleased with you. You have surpassed our greatest expectations. You have saved two worlds, Suvon and your own world. You could not have been aware of this, but three months from now, an unspeakable horror would have crawled through Professor Beauvais' portal, a horror which would have brought an end to all life on your planet."

The room was silent, the friends glancing at each other.

The Sinarian raised one of its long ropey arms, four small silver boxes appearing, hovering in front of him.

"Mrs. Preke shall make the presentations."

Mrs. Preke stepped forward, taking the first silver box, handing it to Odo. "Odo Whitley, it is my distinct honor to welcome you to Peregrin College, and present you with this ring. Well done, Odo. We're so proud of all of you, of everything you have done."

After she had presented each of them with a silver box, she stepped back, saying, "You may open them now."

Odo flipped the box open, eyeing the gold ring with its glowing emerald green stone, the words Peregrin

277

College engraved in a circle around the stone. "A college ring, this is amazing. Thanks, Mrs. Preke!"

Silas was studying his ring. "We still don't know exactly where Peregrin College is."

"It is located in Room 314 PC in the Reiss Science Center at Pravus University. Brochures, letters of acceptance, and class schedules will arrive in the mail shortly, all quite ordinary looking to the uninformed eye. Peregrin College will appear to be a small, but respected college of science, one affiliated with Pravus University. No eyebrows will be raised. Your real classes will be chosen at the beginning of your first semester. "

Silas said, "When Sephie went into Room 314 there was only that infinite blackness, with cracks opening to other times and places."

Professor Ekim nodded. "That would not have been the case had she been wearing her college ring. The empty blackness she found herself in is the Void, the space between dimensions, between universes, between worlds, a gateway to the infinite nows. Your ring is a portal of sorts, creating a defined interdimensional pathway through the Void. When you are wearing your ring, you will step through the door of Room 314 PC onto the campus of Peregrin College, home to over one hundred and fifty-three thousand other students from thousands of different worlds and dimensions, all chosen just as you were."

Silas said, "What happens if we lose our ring, or

someone steals it? Can't they use it to get through the door?"

"The rings are fully synchronized to your biomaps, no one else can use them."

Emmy said. "Um… I'm not as smart as Silas and Odo and Sephie. I can fly, but I don't know much about science. In case you didn't know that, and made a mistake?"

The Sinarian sent out a thought.

"Emmeline Snow, you are far more than you can possibly imagine. This self you call Emmy is only a small temporary part of who you are, and Peregrin College is of a far different nature than any college you are familiar with. We know exactly who and what you are, and that is why you were chosen, why you were given a scholarship."

"When I learned to fly, I merged with Nomi, my deeper self. Is that what you mean?"

"Yes, that was one step in the right direction. Do not doubt yourself, Emmeline Snow."

"Thank you." Emmy looked over at Silas.

"I must leave now, but we shall meet again during your fourth year at Peregrin."

The Sinarian was there, then he was not.

Odo slipped the gold ring onto his finger, a strange tingling sensation flowing through his body. "It feels electric."

Emmy said, "Do Sinarians have names? I didn't know what to call him."

Wikerus said, "They do not. There are many Sinarians, but there is only one Sinarian. It's a rather baffling paradox, fully understood only by the Sinarians."

Odo frowned. "He didn't tell us what the white tiger was."

Professor Ekim smiled. "He is your counselor and guardian. He will help you choose your classes and guide you when necessary."

"My counselor is a tiger?"

"He has chosen to appear in the form of a tiger because his true form would be quite confusing to you. Perhaps bewildering might be a better choice of words."

"So we just show up at Room 314 PC when the brochures and letters tell us to?"

"You may visit the school whenever you wish, now that you have your rings. In fact, it would be best if you visit before the semester begins, so you can get a feel for the school, get used to the wide variety of students attending Peregrin. Rest assured, no matter what their physical form might be, they are quite similar to you in nature."

"Let's rock and roll, boys!"

"You're doing it again. You're stealing my catchphrase."

"I'm not stealing it, you can say it too."

"It doesn't work like that. It sounds ridiculous if two superheroes have the same catchphrase."

Wikerus smiled at Mrs. Preke.

Chapter 42

Out Loud

After thanking Wikerus and Mrs. Preke again, the friends headed back down Expergo Street toward Odo's house.

Emmy was admiring her ring. "This is so amazing. My mom's not going to believe I got a full scholarship to a college."

"I'm still confused. Who was the guy in the tweed suit?"

"Wikerus said he was Professor Ekim. He must teach at Peregrin, or he might be a dean or something."

"That makes sense. I wonder what kind of classes they have there?"

"Probably nothing like classes we'd take here. It must be all super advanced science and stuff."

"The Sinarian made it sound really mysterious, all that stuff about we're far more than we think we are."

"And what's with having a tiger for a counselor?"

"I like tigers."

Silas nodded. "Me too, it sounds fun. Professor Ekim

said the tiger was also our guardian. Does that mean he protects us?"

"Protects us from what?"

"Good question."

Odo stopped short, slapping his hand to his forehead. "No! I don't believe it! No way! This is not going to happen!"

The others turned in surprise. "What's not going to happen?"

"Professor Ekim, that's what's not going to happen. No way am I taking a class from him!"

"Why not? What's wrong with you?"

"What is Ekim spelled backwards?"

"Uh... Mike?"

"Exactly! Professor Ekim is Mike the Mechanic playing one of his dumb tricks on us."

"He didn't look anything like Mike the Mechanic."

"It's him, I know it is. I can smell it. I knew there was something off about him, I knew it. There was a weird look in his eye, like he was laughing."

"We can agree to disagree on that particular point. When do you want to go visit Peregrin College?"

"How about Saturday? We can go in the morning, then to the movies in the afternoon. It's my turn to choose a movie, by the way."

Sephie groaned. "Please don't pick the new Sinister Sorcerer movie."

Emmy said, "See you guys tomorrow. We're going

over to Silas' house."

"See you."

Odo and Sephie turned onto Asper Street, heading toward his house.

Sephie said, "Odo, why do you think Mike the Mechanic would pretend to be an professor at–"

"I love you."

Sephie stopped short. "What?"

"I love you."

"You said it. Out loud. To me."

Odo nodded.

Sephie put her arms around him, holding him close. "I love you too."

"I kind of freaked out when you told us about the Void, thinking about what might have happened if we hadn't been there. I had to tell you."

"I'm glad."

Odo grinned. "Do you really think we've known each other before? Like in other lifetimes and stuff?"

"I know it's true."

The two best friends held hands as they strolled down Asper Street. "Remember in the movie when the bookstore owner told the lady he loved her and you saw me looking at you?"

Sephie snickered. "You should have seen the look on your face. It was so funny, I was trying so hard not to laugh."

They ran up the front steps of Odo's house, Odo

flinging the door open, hollering, "Odo Whitley is in the house!"

His dad called out from the kitchen, "You don't need to yell every time you–" He stopped short when he saw Sephie, an embarrassed look crossing his face.

Petunia waved to her. "Hi, Sephie. How was school today?"

Odo said, "We have something to tell you."

The color drained from Albert's face. "What kind of something to tell us?"

"Nothing much, just that we both got full four-year scholarships to Peregrin College. It turns out it's a super good science and engineering college that's part of Pravus University."

Petunia's jaw dropped. "That's wonderful! I'm so happy for you." She hugged them both. "Congratulations, both of you."

Albert said, "You scared the life out of me. I thought you were going to tell us you were getting married."

"Why would you think that? We're still in high school."

Albert shrugged. "It happens."

Petunia said, "Just ignore him. Sephie, would you like to stay for dinner? We can celebrate."

"I'd love to, I'll just call my mom and tell her."

After a lovely dinner with lots of talk about Peregrin College and a few stories from Albert about the Chocko CrunchCake factory, Sephie headed home, Odo walking her to the door. They stepped outside onto the front porch, Odo leaning over and whispering, "I love you, Sephie Crumb."

Sephie grinned. "See you tomorrow."

Odo headed up to his room, a goofy grin on his face. He was so glad he'd told her, and now he didn't have to worry about it every time he saw her.

He closed his door, stepping over to his desk, eyeing the six large plastic flower pots, each holding a dozen tiny seedlings.

"They're coming along nicely, if they're supposed to have blue and green striped leaves." He grabbed the little bag of orange berry seeds Noran had given him, setting them on his desk.

"I'll keep some of the seeds, and give the rest to Mrs. Beasley, along with all the seedlings. She'll totally win a gold medal for them. Or make a zillion dollars selling orange berry snacks. So delicious."

He sat down at his desk, leaning back in his chair. Only eight more weeks until they graduated, and in the fall they'd be off to a crazy giant college full of aliens. The good news was his best friends in the world would be there with him at Peregrin. Maybe Sephie was right, maybe Professor Ekim wasn't Mike the Mechanic, maybe the name was just a weird coincidence. He jumped up from his chair, peering out the window. The white tiger was standing on the sidewalk across the street.

Odo spotted a man walking down the sidewalk, the tiger directly in his path. "Not good. I hope that tiger doesn't think that guy is–"

The man passed through the tiger as though he wasn't there.

"That was weird." He flopped down on his bed. It didn't get much weirder that having an invisible white tiger for a counselor and guardian. He couldn't wait for Saturday, couldn't wait to visit Peregrin College with Sephie, Silas, and Emmy. It was going to be amazing.

Chapter 43

Dron

"I still can't believe you'll be starting college in the fall. How did our little Odo grow up so fast?"

Odo glanced at Sephie, frowning when he saw the grin on her face. "I'm not exactly your little Odo anymore."

Odo's mom rubbed his shoulder. "I know you're not, and that makes me happy and sad at the same time."

Sephie grinned, "It's going to be so fun. I can't wait to start my engineering classes."

Odo turned when he heard the knock on the front door. "Silas and Emmy are here, we have to go."

"Have fun. I hope you like it."

"We will."

The friends headed to the bus stop, arriving at Pravus University half an hour later.

"Everyone has their Peregrin rings on?"

Silas nodded. "They're super cool except no one's ever heard of Peregrin College. I can't decide if I should major in physics, astrophysics or engineering."

"How about Advanced Nerdology?"

Emmy snickered.

Sephie said, "The classes there might be completely different from anything we're expecting. It's a college full of aliens in another dimension. It's not going to be like Pravus."

"That's a good thing. We can ask about the classes when we get there. I hope it has a nice campus."

They headed for the Reiss Science Center, running up the steps and through the main doors.

Odo whispered, "Let's go check out the secret lab. I want to see if it's still there."

Silas nodded. "Let's do it."

They headed down the hall, turning into a side corridor, stopping when they saw the barricaded wall ahead of them, a large yellow sign blocking their path.

This area closed for renovations.

*Pravus University, Building Yesterday's Brighter
Future for Tomorrow Today*

"They left out the part about kidnapping aliens."

"They won't be doing that anymore."

The friends raced up the stairs to the third floor, looking down the long corridor. "Empty. It's kind of weird how this floor is always empty."

"Not even Professor Ekim is here. Otherwise known as Mike the Mechanic."

Sephie rolled her eyes. "He's not Mike the Mechanic."

"Here we are, Room 314 PC. Who wants to go first?"

Sephie grabbed the door knob, twisting it, swinging the door open, bright sunlight flooding into the hallway.

Four jaws dropped.

"No way."

The four members of the Odd Squad stepped through the doorway onto a vast, sprawling emerald green manicured lawn, wide marble serpentine pathways leading to dozens of stunningly beautiful rounded glass buildings.

"Whoa, those buildings are incredible. They look like art, not buildings. There's not a straight line anywhere, they're all curved, like giant glass bubble buildings."

Emmy grinned. "It's so beautiful. And look at those amazing gardens! Let's go check it out."

As they made their way down the winding marble path, Odo glanced behind them, his eyes on the wooden door hovering above the ground at the end of the path. "Looks like we go back to Pravus through that same door."

"I thought the school would be closed, but there's lots of people here."

Odo eyed three yellow spider creatures strolling along one of the paths. "Not sure if people is the right word."

"Be nice, Odo. The Sinarian said they're just like us."

Emmy gave a screech when a leathery winged creature bearing a startling resemblance to a blue pterosaur landed in front of them. It turned around, studying them curiously.

"You guys freshies?"

"What?"

"Freshies, newbies, you start this fall?"

They nodded.

"Thought so. I had the same look on my face when I first got here. It takes a while to get used to the campus and all the different kinds of students. They're all nice, even though some are pretty strange looking. You guys have your translator disks yet?"

"We have some at home, but I didn't bring any. We just got here. We wanted to see what the school looks like."

The pterosaur made a series of clacking sounds, four small gold disks appearing in his hand.

"Stick these anywhere on your head and everyone will be speaking your language. Not everyone can send non-verbal thoughts. I'm Dron, by the way."

The friends each took a disk.

"Thanks. I'm Silas. We've visited a bunch of different worlds and seen a lot of aliens."

"That's cool, it won't be such a shock then. Wait, are you guys from Earth?"

"We are. Why?"

"I've seen four or five other people here who look like you. Someone said they were from Earth. You're going to have some serious culture shock for the first few months

or so. The technology here is beyond anything you've ever seen. I come from a super high tech world, but this place is way beyond that. I mean, way, way beyond. Crazy stuff."

Odo said, "Are the classes really hard? I haven't had that much physics."

Dron shrugged. *"Don't worry about that, the classes aren't what you're expecting."*

"What are they like?"

"Ever hear of Quantonian physics?"

Odo frowned, shaking his head. He had no idea what it was. He was beginning to wonder if he belonged here.

"Quantonian physics merges Newtonian and Quantum physics into one seamless discipline."

Silas said, "The Theory of Everything?"

"Exactly. Sounds like a scary hard class, right? Trying to learn all that stuff? No need to be scared, the best part about Peregrin is you don't have to study."

"How can you not study?"

Dron made the clacking noises again, a pair of odd looking headphones appearing in his hand.

"These are called Faxx. You wear them during the first week of each class and it uploads all the data into your brain. One week and you'll know everything there is to know about Quantonian physics, and even better, you'll understand it. No studying needed."

"Really?"

"Really. And you never forget it, it's always there,

every word, every formula."

Emmy said, "So what do you do for the rest of the semester?"

"The fun stuff. You use that information to make things, design things, explore new ideas, new theories, create things no one has thought of before."

Silas grinned, "Whoa, that sounds super fun."

"It is. You'll all take Quantonian first semester, probably with Professor Ekim. He's great, a bit eccentric, but cool after you get to know him. He does these weird three question challenge things. They're pretty tough, not the kind of questions you expect. He makes you think, though. Makes you question everything. He's totally brilliant, way past genius."

"I knew it! Professor Ekim is Mike the Mechanic!"

"That's one of his names. You know him?"

"He exists on a whole bunch of worlds at the same time, right?"

"That's the guy. He's a legend, came up with a lot of the theories behind Quantonian physics. Not sure why, but he likes teaching freshies. That's cool you already know him."

"Can we wander around and look at stuff?"

"No problem. A lot of the buildings are closed, but some are open. A bunch of students live here year round, especially ones from dangerous worlds, post apocalyptic stuff. There's some scary bad worlds out there." He studied Sephie's orange hair. *"Fortisian?"*

Sephie nodded. "Half Fortisian."

"You're a shifter?"

"So is Odo."

"Just so you know, you can't shift home from here, you have to take the doors. You can walk through any of the doors and your ring will send you to the right place. It's a security measure. They want to know who's coming and going here. The actual physical location of this place is a highly guarded secret. I don't even know where it is, I just take the doors."

"Why do they keep it a secret?"

"Security. They'll tell you all about that when you start."

"Thanks for talking to us."

"No problem. Maybe I'll see you next semester." He looked at Odo, sending him a thought. *"No worries, you guys totally belong here. All of you."*

Dron spread his wings, soaring up and across the campus.

Silas said, "This place is seriously amazing."

Chapter 44

Pushing Buttons

"Let's go wander around the campus."

"This is a little like Girard Station, there's a zillion kinds of aliens. Look at those praying mantis guys, I remember seeing some of them at Girard Station."

Emmy whispered, "That guy looks like a giant bat walking on three long legs."

"That would be cool to have wings and fly."

"Not as cool as flying like Emmy does."

The friends strolled across the huge campus, stopping to peer into some of the oddly shaped glass buildings.

"Uh… what is that?"

"Goopy green stuff that turns into weird objects and then turns back into goopy green stuff?"

"It can probably form whatever object you tell it to. You could keep some in your backpack, make it transform into whatever you needed, like a flashlight or a cool beam weapon."

"Crazy."

"Look at those blue guys coming out of that big black

294

sphere. I wonder what's in there? I think they're laughing."

"They're all wearing uniforms."

"Maybe everyone on their world wears the same clothes."

"Maybe. Let's go look."

They stepped over to the hundred foot tall black sphere, Odo studying the oval shaped blue door.

"How does it open?"

"I don't see any buttons."

"Try pressing that little raised symbol."

Odo pressed his finger against the curious symbol.

"Nothing."

They spun around when they heard a strange clicking and clacking noise, Odo's eyes widening when he saw the spider creature.

Sephie smiled. "Hi, I'm Sephie."

The clicking noise sounded again.

"I think he's talking."

Emmy whispered, "Use your translator disk."

Odo grabbed his disk, sticking it to his forehead.

"You guys are freshies?"

"We start next semester. We're taking a tour of the campus. It's amazing."

"This is my third year and it's still amazing. You're not going to believe the stuff that goes on here, the tech that gets developed. It's seriously mind boggling."

"What's that goopy green stuff that changes shape?"

The spider laughed. "It's not a what, it's a who."

"That thing's alive?"

"He's working on a formshifting module. When it's done, it will be the size of your watch and you can formshift into anything you want."

"That's crazy."

The spider shrugged. "It's third year stuff. You guys trying to get into the Sphere?"

"We can't figure out how to open the door."

"Touch your ring to the symbol. That's how all the doors open. Your ring has a quantum generated code that activates the door. It lets them know who's going where. Every once in a while we get some bad guys in here. Mostly trying to steal tech, but sometimes a lot worse. You know how to activate your guardian?"

Odo shook his head. "He stands outside my house at night, but I don't know how to make him appear."

"Rap your ring against something, hit it pretty hard. He'll protect you against most anything."

Emmy grinned, smacking her ring against the black sphere, a huge orange lion appearing next to her.

"Cool, that's a creature from your world?"

"It's a lion. He's amazing, I love him."

"Nice. Gotta go, have fun and enjoy your visit. See you next semester."

"Thanks."

When the spider creature was gone, Emmy whispered, "He looked like our old friend Plato. Do you think he's an Argonian?"

"He looked like one. We can ask him next time we see him. Maybe he knows Plato."

"This place is so incredible. I can't believe we're here, and I can't believe we all got scholarships."

Emmy said, "It's amazing how all of us started out thinking there was something wrong with us, and now we're here, at this amazing school. We'll be making things that change worlds."

"Sephie thinks we've all known each other before, in other lifetimes."

Silas nodded. "I talked to some ghosts about that. They were purposefully a little bit vague, but Sephie is right. I'm almost certain that's how it works."

Emmy said, "I wish I could see what we looked like back then."

"Odo probably had horns and scales and giant teeth."

"Very funny. Sounds like a good project for you, goggles that let you see your past lives."

Silas said, "It's not that weird, you'd just be looking back in time, not much different than when we went back in time to Pangaea. The hard part would be finding where and when you had lived before, but there might be a way to track an individual consciousness across time, a kind of temporal fingerprint at a quantum level. Of course, if time is only an illusion, you'd have to–"

"Earth to Silas, it's time to see what's in the big black sphere."

"Maybe it's a snack bar. We can get some lunch."

Sephie touched her ring to the symbol, the door vanishing.

"It worked!" She stepped through, the door solid again.

Silas said, "I guess we each have to do it."

Odo was the last one in, gazing up at the ceiling a hundred feet above him. "It's a big hollow sphere. What's it for?"

"There's a post with lights on it in the center of the room."

They strolled across the cavernous sphere, stopping at a four-foot tall silver cylinder topped with six blinking yellow lights and six violet buttons.

"What is it?" Odo stepped over to the post, eyeing it.

Sephie grabbed his arm. "Don't start pressing buttons. You've seen some of the tech they have here. This could be incredibly dangerous."

"Why would the spider guy let us in if it was dangerous? He knows we're freshies."

"He's not a spider guy, he's an Argonian, and don't push any buttons. I'm serious. Something really bad could happen."

"Those blue guys were in here and they got out okay. They were laughing. Or maybe they were singing, it was kind of hard to tell. They could have been barking."

"It's not funny. We should go."

Before she could stop him, Odo reached out and

pressed the first button. The yellow light turned violet, a black symbol appearing above the light.

"See? Nothing happened."

"Turn it off."

"Fine." Odo tapped it again, the symbol above the light changing. He tapped it nine times, a different symbol appearing each time. "I'm not exactly sure how to turn it off."

Silas said, "Try tapping the next button."

The second light turned violet, a new black symbol appearing.

Emmy said, "Sephie's right, we should go. We don't know what we're doing. We might break something. I don't want to get kicked out of school before we even start."

"They wouldn't have it here if it exploded or something. It can't be a crazy death ray machine, or they wouldn't have any students left. We probably have to press all six buttons."

"What are the symbols for?"

"They must be letters, maybe numbers? It looks like a combination lock, except with weird symbols. When you select six symbols in a certain order, something happens. If you use different symbols, something else happens."

"Time to go."

"Just one second, I want to–"

"Now."

Odo tapped the last four buttons, a shrill alarm sounding, a series of six enormous glowing yellow symbols appearing in the center of the sphere. One by one the symbols changed from yellow to violet, a dreadful rumbling sound filling the air, the ground shaking.

"Odo, what did you do?"

Chapter 45

You Drink

Before Odo had time to answer, they were surrounded by a dense jungle filled with dark blue foliage and buzzing insects.

"What happened? Where are we?"

Sephie was glaring at Odo, her eyes shooting daggers at him.

"Why are you looking at me like that?"

"What did you do? I told you not to push those buttons."

"It's not my fault, I had to push them. I had to know."

Emmy said, "How do we get back? Where's the post with the buttons?"

"I don't see it, it should be right in front of Odo. It's gone."

Silas said, "I think I know what happened. The black sphere is a transport station for students from other worlds. They enter the code for their world, and boom, they're back home. Pretty cool."

Emmy said, "How do we get back to Peregrin?"

"I don't know."

Odo grinned. "No problem, Odo Whitley will save the day. Everyone hold hands and we'll shift back home to Wikerus' house."

Four minutes later Odo said, "I don't understand why it's not working."

"The pterodactyl guy said you can't shift from here."

"Oh, right."

Emmy said, "Are we trapped here? Where is here?"

"We're not trapped. Students use the sphere to commute to Peregrin, so we just have to find a student and ask them how to get there. Easy peasy, Aunt Louisey."

Silas gave him a dubious glance. "And where do we look for this student, exactly?"

"I don't know, maybe a nearby town? This could be a super high tech world, lots of people probably know how to get back."

The four friends ducked down when the dragon creature soared past, high above the treetops, a rush of putrid air hitting them.

"What was that thing? What's that smell? So bad, like burning sulfur."

"It looked like a dragon. That's kind of cool, right? A dragon? That's fun. This isn't so bad."

Sephie pursed her lips, staring silently at Odo.

"Fine, let's go find a village, get directions to the nearest transport station. It shouldn't take long. Let's head toward those mountains."

They forged on through the dense foliage for almost an hour, Silas stopping abruptly, tilting his head. "Do you hear that?"

Emmy said, "It sounds like a steam engine, like Captain Haynes' steamboat in the Land of the Almost Dead."

"Let's go see what it is. A steam engine isn't exactly high tech though."

They turned, heading toward the rhythmic sound, stepping into a wide clearing.

Odo eyed the crudely built wooden shack, a primitive thumping steam engine powering a twenty-foot tall device resembling a small oil rig.

"What is that? Are they drilling for oil?"

Silas stepped over to the hissing, thunking machine, eying the ten foot wide wooden vat next to it, green gelatinous goop glopping out of an iron pipe into the vat. "It's not oil, it's something bad. It smells awful."

"See what it tastes like."

"You first."

They turned when they heard a door creaking open, a dark red serpent creature with four arms slithering out of the wooden shack, a gleaming two bladed axe clutched in its hands.

Silas frowned. "Not a big fan of serpents or giant axes."

Odo called out, "Hi there, can you tell us where the nearest interstellar transport station is?"

The creature stopped, staring at them.

"You are Pintar?"

"No, I'm not Pintar, we're lost, we're trying to find a transport station that will take us back to Peregrin College."

Sephie whispered, "Odo, he has no idea what you're talking about."

The serpent creature lowered the axe, saying, "You will help me. Bring my Ninto home."

Emmy said, "Who is Ninto?"

"My little Ninto, taken by the soldiers."

Odo turned to the others. "I officially apologize for pressing the buttons. Never again, I promise. Never."

Silas waved to the serpent. "We'd love to help you, but we're trying to get home."

"Soldiers take Ninto to Magic City."

"Magic City?"

The serpent nodded. "They take Ninto to Magic City, not come back."

Sephie said, "How far away is Magic City? How long does it take to walk there?"

"Walk there?"

"Yes, how long will it take us to walk to Magic City?"

"No walk, drink Argo."

"What?"

The serpent slithered over to the vat of burbling green goop, grabbing an iron ladle, dipping it into the bubbling glop.

"You drink Argo, go Magic City."

Odo snorted. "Not going to happen, friend. We're not going to drink that stuff and we're not going to Magic City."

Emmy said, "Are you saying if we drink that, it will take us to Magic City?"

"You drink Argo, go Magic City. Find Ninto."

Silas looked at the others. "What do you think it is?"

The serpent bent down, picking up a glass bottle of the green goop, handing it to Sephie. "You tell where go."

"I tell it where I want to go, then drink some?"

"Tell Magic City and drink."

Odo gave a pleasant smile. "Excuse us for one moment."

The friends turned, huddling together, whispering.

"He's clearly trying to poison us. Magic City is probably what they call the afterlife. Drink this and go to the Land of the Almost Dead? I don't think so."

"I don't think he's trying to poison us. It could be some weird alien substance we've never seen before."

"Did you smell that stuff? It can't be good."

"Magic City could be a high tech alien city with transport stations."

"Science that this guy thinks is magic."

"We don't really have any other options."

"Have him drink some first."

"Nice, good idea."

Odo turned to the serpent saying, "Show us how it

works. You drink some of the Argo first."

The serpent nodded. He held the ladle up to his mouth, saying, "Behind strangers."

He took a sip and vanished.

Odo whipped around when he heard the rustling sound, his eyes widening at the sight of the serpent, ladle in hand, standing behind them.

"Whoa, that was crazy. That stuff really works."

Sephie said, "I guess we're going to Magic City."

"I wonder if this stuff would take us back to Peregrin College?"

"Only work here. No home."

Sephie tucked the bottle of green goop into her backpack. "Are we ready?"

Silas said, "Let's rock and roll, boys."

"You're using Sephie's new catchphrase."

"No, mine is, see you later boys, I have a world to save."

"Oh, right. This catchphrase thing is so confusing. Let's just go."

Silas stepped over to the serpent. "We'll go to Magic City, find Ninto."

The serpent handed Silas a small silver whistle.

"What is this?"

"Blow whistle, Ninto come."

"Thanks, that should help."

"You bring Ninto back, I help you."

"You'll help us get back to Peregrin College?"

"Bring Ninto back, I help you." The serpent raised the ladle, saying, "Magic City."

One by one the adventurers took a sip, and one by one they vanished.

Chapter 46

Today's Password

Odo stood gaping at the six towering skyscrapers sparkling in the bright sunlight. "This place is crazy. Look how tall the buildings are."

Silas said, "I don't get it, they have super high tech glass buildings, but they're riding around on those big furry rabbit creatures? They should have grav cars."

Emmy said, "The rabbit creatures are pulling carriages. That seems kind of cruel."

"I never thought I'd see a serpent riding on a giant rabbit. Nice saddle though, fancy."

"Check out those lizard guys over there. They have swords, and they don't exactly look friendly."

"They're totally scary. That one guy has scars all over him. They look like soldiers, maybe some kind of elite guard."

Emmy whispered, "One of them is looking at us."

The badly scarred lizard stepped across the cobblestone street, approaching the four friends.

"Identify yourself, strangers."

"I'm Odo Whitley."

"Your world of origin?"

"Earth."

"What is the purpose of your visit to Magic City?"

"We're helping a friend, trying to find someone called Ninto."

"Beelor the Argo farmer?"

"Maybe, I don't know his name, he just said soldiers came and took his Ninto."

"I see." The guard pulled out a small pad of paper, turning away from Odo, writing something in the pad.

"You are free to go. Good luck to you, and welcome to Magic City."

"Do you know Beelor the Argo farmer?"

The lizard nodded. "He is an old friend of mine."

"What does Ninto look like?"

The lizard guard tapped a jeweled bracelet on his wrist, a slowly rotating holographic image of a six-legged furry animal with a long white tail appearing in front of Odo. "Ninto is Beelor's pet grindle."

"You have holograms here? Why do people ride those big rabbit creatures?"

"You are free to go now." The guard turned, heading back to his friends.

Odo said, "Ninto is a six-legged cat thing with a long white tail."

"We're looking for a lost cat? How are we going to get home?"

"We have to take Ninto back to Beelor the Argo Farmer. Why did I push those stupid buttons? What's wrong with me?"

Sephie put her arm around him. "There's nothing wrong with you, you're just curious. But don't do it again. Ever."

Silas said, "Being curious is a good thing. You can't be a good scientist if you're not curious."

"Try blowing the whistle."

Silas put the silver whistle to his lips, blowing it, a barely audible high pitched sound filling the air.

Moments later a six-legged cat creature stepped out from a shadowy doorway.

"It worked!"

Seven more cat creatures stepped out of doorways, the friends soon surrounded by three dozen of the chattering furry creatures.

"This is great, now what?"

Emmy got down on her knees. "Ninto, Ninto, come here, buddy."

The cat creatures swarmed over her.

"Aggh, get them off me!"

Odo said, "This is crazy, how are we supposed to find this dumb cat?"

"Beelor the Argo Farmer said the soldiers took Ninto. We need to find some soldiers and ask them if they've seen him."

Silas said, "I'm going to go talk to the lizard guard

again."

He returned three minutes later, a frown on his face. "See that shiny thing up on top of the mountain?"

Odo squinted, trying to focus on it. "What is it?"

"It's called The Crystal Castle. The king lives up there and so do all his soldiers."

"Seriously? We have to climb a mountain to some weird Crystal Castle and talk to the king? All I want to do is go back to Peregrin."

Sephie pulled out the glass bottle of Argo, removing the wooden stopper. "We don't need to climb the mountain."

"Nice, great idea."

Emmy pulled a plastic spoon from her pack. "Use this."

Sephie poured Argo into the spoon, saying, "The Crystal Castle." She grinned at Odo. "Open wide, button pusher."

She spooned the liquid into Odo's mouth and he vanished. When Sephie arrived, the others were gazing up at the imposing massive crystalline structure.

"This place is incredible. Look how big it is, all those towers. So cool how it sparkles in the sunlight. How do you think they built it?"

"There's no way they could mine that much crystal, it has to be a synthetic material."

"I don't understand how they can be so high tech and primitive at the same time. They can build a synthetic crystal castle, but they still ride around on giant rabbits?"

"There's the entrance." Odo pointed to a wide silver drawbridge.

"What are those things swimming in the moat?"

"They look like crocodiles with wings."

"Just what we need, flying crocodiles."

"It could be worse, they could be flying monkeys."

"Why would flying monkeys be swimming in a moat?"

The friends strolled across the bridge, a stern looking guard holding up his hand, motioning for them to stop.

"What is the purpose of your visit to the Crystal Castle?"

"We need to speak to the soldiers about a missing grindle named Ninto."

The guard took out a small pad, writing something on it. "You may pass. Soldiers are stationed on the second sublevel. Enter through the keep. Today's password is *crystal.*"

"Thanks."

The four friends stepped through the gatehouse into the main castle yard. "This place is crazy. Those towers must be two hundred feet tall."

"There's the keep. We go in there."

They strode across the grass toward the keep doors, stopping when a surly castle guard held up his hand.

"Today's password?"

Emmy said, "Today's password is *crystal.*"

"INCORRECT!" The guard pulled out a deadly looking short sword.

"The other guard just told us today's password was *crystal*."

The guard blew a gold whistle, its shrill sound reverberating across the yard. There was a rumbling sound, a twenty-foot tall gleaming metallic warrior appearing out of nowhere, an enormous sparkling gold sword in his hand.

The guard gave a smirky grin. "Defeat Drogor and you may enter the keep."

"Are you serious? How are we supposed to defeat that thing?"

The guard stepped into the keep, closing the heavy crystal doors behind him.

Drogor raised his sword, stomping one foot, the ground shaking. "DROGOR KILL!"

Sephie drew a quick symbol, the friends surrounded by a shimmering defensive energy field.

"What do we do?"

Odo said, "Beam gun!"

Sephie drew three symbols, a deadly looking black weapon appearing.

"Look for a weak spot!"

"Shoot his leg, maybe he'll fall over!"

Sephie fired the beam gun, the blast of light bouncing off the huge metal warrior. "It's not working! It bounces right off him!"

Drogor raised his sword. "DROGOR KILL!"

"RUN!"

The friends turned to run, Odo tripping and falling on a loose tile, letting out a terrified screech when he saw the gleaming gold blade flashing down toward him. This was the end, and it was all his fault, he was the one who pushed those stupid buttons.

His world went black when the sword hit him.

"We're closing in five minutes. You'll have to come back tomorrow."

Odo staggered to his feet, looking around. He wasn't dead, this was good. Was he in the Void? The Land of the Almost Dead? He squinted in the darkness, spotting Sephie. She was standing in front of a tall praying mantis creature.

He heard Silas say, "What happened?"

"We're closing, you can come back tomorrow. We're open from eight until four during semester breaks."

Odo looked around, his eyes adjusting to the dim light. They were in the black sphere. "How did we get back here?"

"Get back here?"

"We were in another world, a big robot guy was trying to kill us with a giant gold sword."

The praying mantis glanced at the cylinder with its six buttons and lights. "You were playing Crystal Castle? How did you like it?"

"We were playing Crystal Castle?"

"Not my favorite, kind of boring. The story is full of holes, and you don't even see Ninto until level sixteen. The bosses are ridiculously hard and they're all the same, they all look like Drogor. Alien Apocalypse is a way better game. Super fun, you should try it."

"That was a game?"

The praying mantis studied them curiously. "Wait, are you freshies?"

"We start next semester."

He smiled. "You thought it was real."

Odo gave an embarrassed grin. "We thought this was a portal to other worlds."

"Don't feel bad, you're not the first freshies to think that. Freshies come in here all the time and start pushing buttons. When the school is open, this is the World Sim Center, with realistic simulations of thousands of real worlds. It's used to prepare students for missions. During semester break we put games on it and call it the Sphere. Oh, if you want to end the game, just press your ring and say 'game over'."

Silas said, "What kind of missions are they preparing us for?"

"They're all different. They'll tell you about it first semester. I have to go. You guys know how to use the doors to get home?"

Odo nodded.

They stepped out into the bright sunlight, Odo looking at the others. "That was terrifying. I thought I was toast when I saw Drogor coming at me with that giant gold sword. No more button pushing, I promise."

Silas nodded. "It was super scary. We should come back tomorrow and play Alien Apocalypse."

Sephie grinned. "Let's do it."

ONE YEAR LATER

Odo got up from his desk, twisting the glowing emerald gem on his Peregrin ring, a voice sounding in his head.

"Where are you? The movie starts in ten minutes."

"Be right there."

He tapped his ring and vanished, his shimmering ethereal form appearing in front of the movie theater, Sephie waving to him.

He floated over to Sephie. "Where are Emmy and Silas?"

"They couldn't make it, they're working on a project at school, the solar powered disforming disk. We're on our own today." She glanced around to see if anyone was watching. "You're good to go."

Odo tapped his ring, turning solid. "It's your turn to buy snacks, you know."

"What time is your mom's graduation?"

"Three o'clock on Saturday."

"Wear something nice."

"I was thinking I could wear my cool adventuring coat."

"Or not."

"Fine, I'll wear something nice. Oh, Mrs. Beasley got

her check from the Global Health Foundation yesterday." Odo leaned forward, whispering, "Six *million* dollars."

"Her arthritis never came back?"

"The orange berries totally cured it. The Foundation is shipping free seeds all over the world. No more arthritis. They think the berries will cure a lot of other stuff too."

"You were lucky, those berries could have turned everyone into crazy killer zombies."

"You stole that joke from Silas. He still thinks it would make an amazing movie."

"I didn't steal his joke, I borrowed it. We should go, the movie starts in five minutes."

"Which one did you pick?"

"It's a romantic one, but I think you'll like it, it has lots of action and adventure. It's about a shy translucent boy who falls in love with an orange haired alien girl. She's beautiful, but doesn't know it, and she has amazing powers. He's afraid to talk to her at first, but he finally tells her he loves her."

Odo laughed. "That sounds strangely familiar. Does the orange haired girl love the shy translucent boy?"

"She does. More than he will ever know."

Odo put his arm around her. "It sounds totally amazing. They live happily ever after, right?"

"Let's go find out, Odo Whitley."

"Best adventure ever, Sephie Crumb."

If you enjoyed reading
*The Translucent Boy and the
Children of Ice*
please leave a short review or rating
on Amazon.com
Reviews are the lifeblood of indie publishers –
we can't survive without them!

If you have any comments or suggestions
or would like to be notified of upcoming book
releases and Free Kindle book day promotions,
please email me at
OrvilleMouse@gmail.com

Follow me at:
www.facebook.com/TomHoffmanAuthor/

Best wishes until we meet again,

Tom Hoffman

ABOUT THE AUTHOR

Tom Hoffman received a B.S. in psychology
from Georgetown University
and a B.A. from the now-defunct
Oregon College of Art. He has lived in Alaska
with his wife since 1973. They have two
adult children and three adorable
grandchildren. Tom was a graphic designer
and artist for over 35 years.
Redirecting his imagination from art to
writing, he wrote his first novel,
The Eleventh Ring, at age 63.